THE SONG OF YOUTH

Montserrat Roig (Barcelona, 1946-1991) was a novelist, short story writer, investigative journalist and feminist activist, described by the poet Marta Pessarrodona as the 'first female total writer Catalan literature has had.' She is widely regarded as forming a central part of the Catalan canon and has inspired generations of writers in her native Catalonia to seek the intimate, personal testimonies of ordinary people within a wider vision of history guided by a strong sociopolitical engagement. Left-wing, feminist politics, a commitment to the Catalan language, the use of the written word as a weapon against 'dismemory' and the complexities of the self are themes that she explored throughout her career, which was cut tragically short by illness. She was the recipient of the Premi Víctor Català, the Premi Sant Jordi, the Premi Crítica Serra d'Or and the Premi Nacional de Literatura Catalana.

Tiago Miller (London, 1987) is a writer and translator living and working in Lleida, Catalonia. In addition to Montserrat Roig, he has translated Raül Garrigasait, Pere Calders and Manuel de Pedrolo. He has also contributed articles on Catalan culture and language to *Núvol*, *La República* and other publications.

FUM D'ESTAMPA PRESS LTD.
LONDON – BARCELONA
WWW.FUMDESTAMPA.COM

This translation has been published in Great Britain
by Fum d'Estampa Press Limited 2021

001

El cant de la joventut by Montserrat Roig

Printed and bound by TJ Books Ltd, Padstow, Cornwall
A CIP catalogue record for this book is available from the British Library

ISBN: 978-1-913744-02-1

Series design by 'el mestre' Rai Benach

This work was translated with the help of a grant from the Institut Ramon Llull.

Catalan Language and Culture

FUM D'ESTAMPA PRESS

THE SONG OF YOUTH

MONTSERRAT ROIG

Translated by
TIAGO MILLER

To Maria Isabel Roig

THE SONG OF YOUTH

To Doctors Nolasc Acarín and August Andrés

I turn my face from the ominous day,
Before it comes, everlasting night,
So lifeless, it's long since passed away.

But shimmering faith renews my fight;
And I turn, with joy, towards the light,
Along galleries of deepest memory.
        JOSEP CARNER, *Absence*

She didn't squeeze her eyes shut, she just let them rest. She did it every morning, before the nurse began her rounds. She liked having them closed like that, as if they were covered by a sheer silk scarf. Rose pink. Then she'd slowly open her eyes and see that everything was still in its place. She opened them because she wanted to, just like she could move her hands or turn her head a little if she wished. She looked up and saw the milky morning light coming in through the window, slumbersome still. There were the lifeless, white walls and, in the middle of the room, the folding screen. Yes, everything was still in its place. The objects woke up with her. There they were once again, after the short night. Hospital nights are always short.

She listened to the laboured breathing of the woman behind the folding screen. It was hoarse and heavy, as if a machine were sitting on her chest. A death rattle. Since they had moved her to that room, the woman behind the screen would be the fourth to die. Her breaths would grow increasingly frail and further apart, until daybreak would arrive and she wouldn't hear anything more. They all died at daybreak. Just like the night. The doctor in the ward once told her that it was due to cortisol, the stress hormone. That was why she liked to feel her eyelids resting upon her eyes before slowly opening them and checking that everything was still in its place. She never said anything to the women they put behind the screen. They wouldn't have heard her anyway. Bodies don't have anything to say to one another, although she always tried to breathe at a different rate. For every breath the other made, she made two. She filled her lungs with oxygen, as if down to the very pit of her stomach, and then let the air out, softly, rhythmically, through her nose. No, nothing connected her to the body behind the screen. They were merely two coeval creatures. The bodies of two old women moved from the ward to the room on the upper floor to die there. Some died in a hurry, while others took a little longer.

She was one of those that took longer. When she felt the gentle caress of her eyelids, that rose-coloured veil separating her from the objects in the room, from the window, the walls, the screen, she knew she was alive. The breathing of the old woman next to her grew more distant, as did the clanking of the cleaner's mop bucket and the rumbling of the breakfast trolley moving along the corridor. Ever since her attack, when a great gulp of blood had seemingly lodged itself in her brain, she heard a buzzing, a distant hum, which at times took on the form of a melody. It was a song. A group of young hikers had been singing it. "*Tomorrow belongs to me…*" it began. She never heard it again, only that Sunday in the bar while she sipped vermouth with her parents after Mass. She began to laugh.

'Well, it sure looks like we're in a good mood today, doesn't it?'

The doctor, having just entered the room, shot her an ironic glance. He never spoke to her in that overly familiar way, like that awful nurse. But the young-man-in-white's visits were far too fleeting. She couldn't hold onto him. With each breath he got further away.

'I'm not planning on kicking the bucket just yet, even if you are short of beds,' she answered, her eyes wide open now.

'Oh, Zelda, you and your jokes,' said the doctor as he

disappeared behind the screen.

Not even today could she hold onto the doctor's white back with her gaze. A broad back with slightly square shoulders. Like the back waiting with such composure at the bar. A stranger's back. Wearing a white shirt. He'd walked in without looking at anyone, a decisive air about him. The men who came from the war didn't have that air. Lluís, for example, would bury his face in her breasts while she stroked his head like a little boy. He, on the other hand, stood motionless at the bar, not once turning around. His hair was black, slightly curly, and came halfway down the back of his neck. Just like the doctor's.

A ray of sunshine crept through the window and illuminated the specks of dust as they danced uniformly along the line of yellow light before floating past the folding screen and falling dead to the floor. The doctor brushed past the corner of the screen with his left shoulder. She couldn't lift herself up to see all of the doctor's white back. When she saw the stranger's shirt at the bar she lowered her gaze. But even if she couldn't see it, she could sense it, just like the back of his neck, so taut and still. A wild animal ready to pounce. She felt her legs turn to steel.

'So, princess, did we have a good night last night?' asked the nurse, a blood pressure monitor in one hand, a thermometer in the other.

'I'm not dead yet, if that's what you mean. As for yours, I've no idea. How do you expect me to know?'

'I see we're happy this morning...'

'There you go again! Must you say 'we' all the time?'

'It's a figure of speech, sweetheart... Now, I'll just pop in the thermometer and...'

'You should speak to the dying with more respect.'

She heard the doctor murmur something to his assistant. She didn't need to hear the words to know what it meant: the fourth woman wouldn't make it past early morning.

'Now, you take those little pills the doctor prescribed you

when you had your funny turn.'

'You feel put out I'm not dead yet, don't you?'

'Why, you're as strong as an oak.'

'Old trees die a slow death.'

The doctor had since appeared from behind the screen and was now in conversation with his assistant. The nurse still hadn't raised her pillows and she couldn't see the doctor's full figure from her horizontal position. He turned and looked at her without seeing her. The man at the bar, on the other hand, most definitely had; he'd seen her as he turned around, one elbow leaning on the bar and a tumbler of wine in his hand. That time, she didn't lower her eyes and instead returned his stare. He had a big forehead and wore his hair slicked back. Hair that shone. He didn't smile, he didn't speak to anyone. His large hand was clasped firmly around the glass of wine. She felt as if someone were squeezing her heart, forcing it up and out of her mouth. Diabolical, she thought.

Now the nurse and the assistant were talking while the doctor listened with his eyes fixed upon her. At the bar her parents also talked about something or other, while he stood there staring at her as if they were the only two in the room. She didn't hear what her parents were saying, only the hum of the hikers' distant song. The moment he looked at her, she knew what he wanted. And what he wanted, she couldn't tell anyone.

'Now, don't worry yourself this afternoon, princess,' said the nurse. 'The priest will be popping in to say hi to your friend.'

'I can't stand priests,' she murmured. 'Always dressed in black.'

'Well, of course they are! But that doesn't mean anything. Don't tell me you're superstitious...'

'Only those who sniff out death dress in black.'

'Oh, come off it! Don't tell me you're a nonbeliever!'

'That's none of your business.'

'You really are an impossible old woman,' muttered the

nurse. 'It's enough to make Job lose his patience! Anyway, if you're not a good girl, we won't be taking you back downstairs to the ward.'

At the bar, she got up to go to the toilet. Passing just a metre from where he was standing, she felt naked as she walked by. She looked at herself in the mirror and saw a different person reflected back at her. She washed her hands three times. She sprinkled perfume under her arms. She wanted her whole body to smell of lavender. The toilet door creaked open and the white shirt appeared. She turned the tap to wash her hands again, but he stopped her. His large hand clasped her wrist, just as it had the glass of wine before. She let him do it and felt a torrent rush through her. He pulled her into him as water dripped from the tap. At first she raised her arms, as if trying to grab onto thin air, before relaxing and lowering them softly onto his white back. 'Shh,' he whispered. She closed her eyes as both bodies plunged towards an earthy, fiery depth.

Behind the screen, the fourth woman's breathing sounded like the whistling of a tired train. The doctor was still looking at her without seeing her, while the others said words like 'family', 'documents' and 'bed.' A triangle, a word in each angle, and within, the doctor's reproachful eye. She burst out laughing. The nurse spun around angrily.

'What are you smirking at now?'

'Nothing.'

'It really gets on my nerves that laugh of yours. Anyway, if you laugh your blood pressure will go up. And you know it's not good for you. And then who'll have to come running, huh? As if we didn't have enough on our plate already.'

Through the window she could make out a sliver of blue sky. The doctor left and the specks of dust danced in two parallel lines again. The dust dances before turning to ash, she thought, and turned her head the other way. She didn't want to see the ray of sunlight. She didn't want to see the folding screen. She let him squeeze her tightly as she rested her ear upon the white shirt, boom-boom went her heart, and she watched the white tiles gyrate with them. Everything was one: the beating of her heart, the white of the shirt, the white of the tiles. One and everlasting. But the dance was over when he bit her ear and she saw tiny red lines appear in the whites of his eyes.

'Now, you have a little sip of orange juice and afterwards we'll sit you up a bit,' said the nurse.

'When will the doctor be back?'

'What do you want the doctor for? He's already seen you. And he said that if you behave, perhaps you'll be able to go back down to the ward.'

'I'm fine here.'

'Now, now, princess,' replied the nurse as she plumped up the pillows and took the bedpan out from under her. 'Don't be silly. We'll take you back downstairs. We'll get you sitting in a chair. You can move your hands. You might even go back to eating by yourself and everything.'

'And what if I want to die?'

'You know very well that here we don't let anyone die. We die when it's our time.'

He told her the time. Six o'clock. At six I'll be waiting for you, at the bottom of the path that leads up to the vineyards. The toilet door closed behind his white back and the tiles returned to their place. She took her time before emerging. She did her hair and the mirror reflected a pair of reddened eyes back at her. She burst into tears, full of a wild joy. She cried while contemplating herself in the mirror. She liked her new face, she realised she was pretty. Her parents were standing in the middle of the bar waiting for her, ready to go home. She heard her father say something about 'documents and family', while her mother added they would have to 'buy a new bed.' After lunch, Lluís would be coming over with his parents to finalise the wedding arrangements. He had three days' leave.

She raised a hand and held it against the ray of sunlight coming in through the window. It was a transparent hand with protruding bones, riddled with swollen blue rivers cut through by clods of earth coloured stains. Then she held it by the wall. The hand was no longer as transparent. When we get old, she thought, our bones seem to have a life of their own. My skeleton is trying to burst through my skin. But, as thin as it may be, it's the only thing stopping me from being what I really am: grotesque. It's hard to believe that our bodies are made up mostly of water. No, not water. It's jelly.

She listened to the fourth woman wheeze more slowly now, her hand still held next to the peeling paint. She saw a hand stretched towards a sun depositing its fiery dregs along the jagged crests before it disappeared beyond the mountains. The skin was still elastic then. There was fat underneath it. It wasn't like wrinkled leather. Lluís kissed her hand before leaving. 'In three weeks you'll be my wife. I love you.' The slate soil made for darker puddles where the uppermost vineyards grew. 'I want you,' he said as they lay down among the vines. The path up to the vineyards was long. She'd gone up there by bicycle, listening to her heart pound from the tips of her toes up to her brain. The vines formed parallel lines, just like the rays of sunlight that made the dust dance. A landscape of vines that almost kissed the peaks. 'Shh...' he whispered once again.

She smoothed down the hem of the sheets with both hands before suddenly clenching them, remembering a youthful hand whose skin still hid the bones. She felt the sopping wet white shirt on top of her and saw the glistening vines stretching in two parallel lines towards infinity. A body that was becoming hers. She was he. 'Where are you from?' she asked when he was inside her. 'Hell.' A cloud covered the sun and the room fell into darkness. That very evening, he told her, he was to go back to the front. Hearing those words, she tore open his shirt and dug her nails hard into his back.

'Do you think we're going to make your bed for you all day?' howled the nurse. 'Just look what you've done! We're not here to wait on you!'

'Get lost.'

'You really are a wicked old woman.'

'I don't want to die.'

The fourth woman agreed and responded with a high-pitched whistle that gradually grew fainter like a train reaching its final stop. The nurse disappeared behind the screen. Then she rushed out of the room.

'You don't want to die either, huh?'

But now no sound came from the other side of the screen. The ray of sunshine appeared again and the dust began a different dance. The nurse returned with a young man dressed in black. They both vanished behind the folding screen and she heard the whisper of that same triangle of words: 'family', 'documents', 'bed'. The fourth woman didn't die at daybreak after all. This time, she thought, the theory of the stress hormone had failed.

She watched the young-man-in-black's shoulders brush past the corner of the screen. He murmured something to the nurse. The young-man-in-black turned towards her and smiled sweetly with a timid air and a tender look in his eyes. He began to walk towards the bed, as if he had something urgent to tell her. But she closed her eyes and, in doing so, made all of the objects in the room disappear. The path to the upper vineyards was long. Above the peaks, a dazzling ball of fire was blinding her. The climb was tough, there was no air, she gasped for breath. Her heart no longer pounded in her feet, only in her brain. She had to remember something. Remember. Remember a word. If not, she would die.

The young-man-in-black touched her on the shoulder.

'Now it's you who needs me,' he said to her joyfully.

She took a deep breath. The hand still sat on her shoulder. It was heavy. She turned her head slightly and opened her eyes.

'Shh,' he whispered.

She tried to trap the buzzing, that distant hum which at times took on the form of a melody. But the song had become lost among the objects in the room.

'The passing of her neighbour must have given her a fright,' said the nurse while taking her blood pressure. 'We'll have to put her in the bed behind the screen.'

'Does she have any family?'

'I don't think so. Her documents are in the office. I think she's widowed.'

'Di-a-bo-li-cal,' she murmured, breathing deeply between each syllable.

The hand relaxed its grip.

'What did she say?' asked the young man in black.

'I don't know... We'll have to call the doctor.'

'That's it,' she said, before laughing silently to herself.

LOVE AND ASHES

Spiderlike, I spin mirrors,
Loyal to my image.
    SYLVIA PLATH, *Childless Woman*

Maria wasn't aware she had dreams until Marta spoke of hers. Maria was what they call a 'happy' woman and everyone found her to be kind-hearted; her dreams, however, were like the lizards snoozing under the stones in the summer. Marta observed Maria with a certain pity, unsure of how to tell her that there was a whole world out there, just waiting. Each summer, Marta and her husband would travel to countries with strange-sounding names and return with an armful of slides, which they showed to friends on Sunday afternoons. Maria – who Marta never failed to invite over – associated those early evenings with the taste of chocolate.

Maria couldn't stand chocolate. It reminded her of the prolonged penitence of First Communion. She much preferred the tickle of champagne, served in tall glasses, the ones that clink when you say 'chin chin'. But she didn't say any of that to Marta; she was a kind-hearted woman, after all. Marta and her husband told Maria and her husband stories of lost cities in the jungle, impassable rivers later discovered by gold prospectors, pink marble mausoleums and heavenly paradises, and Maria listened to Oriental tales that told of doomed loves, lost shipwrecks and remarkable deaths. As Marta spoke, Maria felt the furrows on her forehead deepen: the deaths she had known were far too homespun to be narrated.

Maria found that each trip made Marta more beautiful, more knowledgeable, more complete, as if an angel had made her anew, and she'd glide as weightless as the desert clouds. Marta poetically embellished her husband's laconic phrases as she poured Maria another small cup of hot chocolate. Marta knew perfectly well that Maria detested chocolate.

Maria washed ten times a day. She was convinced her husband didn't kiss her anymore because she smelt bad. She'd read it in a magazine: once a woman was past forty her kisses smelt rotten. She thought her body had become mouldy on the inside, like a stale room where the sun never entered. Perhaps the foul smell started when the doctor told her she couldn't have children. The blood that flowed out each month felt more like refuse to her, serving no purpose, as useless as the rotten smell. And it was for that reason, she thought, there was no love or money in their life.

But one day everything changed. Her husband arrived home and planted a kiss on the back of her neck, freeing Maria from the oppressive taste of chocolate. He kissed the back of her neck, just like he used to, and she felt a surge run along her spine. Her body stiffened and her skin became firm. It was a surge simultaneously soothing and unnerving. 'Look', her husband told her, 'even poor folk like us can travel these days. Before I die, I want to see where the giraffes roam.' He then showed her a brightly-coloured brochure. Maria saw two camels gazing back at her with their pin-like eyes and gently flared nostrils, both of them seeming to say: 'do it.' 'They're nodding,' she said to herself. Once again, she felt her spine tingle and her skin tense. Then she was seeing the undulating yellow of the desert sands, markets that awaken fears and reveal secrets, elephants crossing rivers with the slowness of the centuries and golden mosques that dazzle like a czarina's ark.

Maria's husband placed a pale forefinger on the page: 'this is where we're going, to the Samburu Reserve, beyond Mount Kenya, towards the forbidden lands. I want to see the reticulated giraffes.'

Everything happened in a hurry. Maria's husband asked for a bank loan and she pawned her grandmother's jewellery. She no longer smelt anything when he turned his back at night. Her body didn't smell rotten and the cells of sadness in her brain had been extinguished. She glided down the stairs like a bride and smiled at the checkout girl. Maria was a woman with hope. She'd never given reticulated giraffes a thought; truth be told, she wasn't even aware of their existence. But now she had the same dreams as Marta: she dreamt about the day they would leave the cases at the door, the day they would arrive home loaded up with images and words, the Sunday afternoons, and the tall champagne glasses, the ones that clink.

Her husband bought a slide projector and a new camera; Maria, the lingerie she'd always dreamt of. She stood before the mirror dressed in the black, satin slip with its lace trim, her naked back revealed by a deep décolletage, and contemplated the skin of the woman gazing back at her. They both began to caress themselves. Neither of them smelt bad.

The first couple of days left only a few fleeting memories. She lived entirely for their return. Everything was new, it went by in a flash, and was all too easy to forget. One night, she watched the full moon rise like a silver balloon. She waited for her husband into the cold hours of early morning. The wait, however, wasn't like before, made up of dead, empty time. She finally drifted off at dawn when nature begins to raise its sleepy head. He woke her gently and caressed a hand over the satin slip. His fingers glided towards her naked back and lingered there. 'Darling,' he said softly, 'today's the day we're going to see the reticulated giraffes.'

The animal stared at them through slit-like eyes with eternal indifference. Maria's husband was in a frenzy. 'Look at it!' he said. 'Take a good look at it because you'll never see a reticulated giraffe again!' Maria and the giraffe looked long and hard at one another with silent intensity, their eyes melting into the same deep, meditative gaze, until finally the animal shook its head and galloped away.

For an instant, it seemed to Maria that the giraffe was like the woman in the mirror and that its eyes expressed the sorrow she no longer felt.

Maria's husband ordered a handler to catch the giraffe. The

handler lassoed it and the animal fell to its knees. That was when Maria's husband hauled himself up onto its hindquarters while the handler shrieked something unintelligible. Maria's husband, giggling like a child, called out for his wife to prepare the camera. 'Not everyone's been photographed riding a reticulated giraffe!' he bellowed. Maria focused on him before squeezing her eyes shut to retain the image. Her husband, however, kept on hollering, 'The camera, the camera!' Meanwhile, the giraffe gently swayed back and forth before raising and then straightening its neck with ancient elegance. 'The cam…!' But this time he didn't get to finish the word. The giraffe shook its hindquarters, freeing itself from the intruder. The fall was fatal. He was instantly as limp as a ragdoll, his neck snapped in two, a latent lament in his eyes. The giraffe looked at the sky and Maria looked at the ground: her husband had lost a shoe.

The consul in Nairobi warned Maria of the expense involved in repatriating the body, given the travel agency didn't cover such costs. He did, however, offer her a solution: they could cremate the poor soul and she could take the ashes home with her. They returned her husband in a flask with a label attached to it. Maria checked the name and confirmed everything was in order. Back at the hotel, she emptied the finely-polished crystal jar of bath salts and began to pour in the remains. When she was done, she placed the jar next to the creams and the hand soap. The other travellers in the group offered their condolences and wished her farewell. But she wasn't wishing anyone farewell. She'd paid for the trip upfront and, anyway, she told herself, money wasn't like blood, flowing freely, month after month. At night, she would get into bed dressed in the satin slip and place the jar behind her, almost touching her bare back.

And then she'd begin to speak.

She told him everything she'd seen during the day: the dance of the zebras; the march of the elephants; how the wind whistled down from the forbidden hills; the starless nights; and the iridescent birds spiralling upwards until they merged with the infinite sky, a sky so blue it hurt. One night, she even told him she'd seen the reticulated giraffe, running freely.

Maria returned home with just a single story to tell, selected in a moment of love: the memory of her husband sat upon the reticulated giraffe and his voice that said 'take a good look at me and preserve me forever.' No camera had captured the image so no one believed it.

Married again and happy, Maria is a kind-hearted woman. She smells her body and notes hints of oleander. From time to time, she shuts herself in the bathroom and sips champagne with the woman in the mirror. They raise their glasses in a silent toast and look lovingly over at a finely-polished crystal jar.

FREE FROM WAR AND WAVE

For Roger

The others, escaping a watery grave,
Were finally free from war and wave.
    The Odyssey, BOOK I

...it is likely best that we no longer meticulously
describe the greatest man of his day, or indicate
the most celebrated in the past but, instead, we
should take the same great pains to relate the
unique existences of men, whether they were
divine, mediocre, or criminal.
    MARCEL SCHWOB, *Imaginary Lives*

'His mother,' Iris explained to me one sleepless night, 'owned a tavern in the Gothic quarter of the small city, close to the cathedral. The soldiers would visit her when they had leave, and even a colonel – not quite so sleazy as far as colonels go – warmed himself between her sheets on those cold winter mornings when the fog lay low and blocked out the sun until noon. Biel wasn't yet three when he'd curl up under the bar and contemplate his mother's shoes. If she'd put on the ones with the golden heels and silver trim, he'd keep a wide berth, for that meant she'd spent the night with the colonel. If she was wearing sandals, it meant his mother had slept with the flute-playing shepherd and she'd have a face like thunder all day.'

'What's this? Some sort of rural drama?' I asked Iris while feigning a yawn.

'If you'd read Víctor Català's *Solitude* – which you haven't, of course – you'd at least have some idea of what the flute symbolises,' she answered.

*Translation by Chris Clarke

'A symbol only a critic without much imagination would dredge up… Anyway, *do* go on.'

'The days she shuffled around, treading down the backs of her slippers, meant she felt repentant: she'd been with the priest. This priest, who'd later be murdered during the civil war, was from another city beyond the valley and he'd bring Biel hazelnuts and honey. If he was really in a good mood he read him passages from *The Odyssey*. But he never got past Book 1: he was always in a hurry.

'One day, his mother was late in coming downstairs. When she finally appeared, she was sporting a slipper on one foot and a sandal on the other. Biel knew just by looking at her feet that she'd been crying. Slowly, he emerged from under the bar and saw she was wearing a long necklace, wrapped three times around her neck. It was a present from the colonel. He was being sent to Africa. Before leaving, he gave Biel his kepi and a brass medal.

'When the soldiers disappeared, the actors came. They brought with them the popular plays from Barcelona, stayed up late into the night and drank only the finest wines. His mother stopped wearing her silver-trimmed shoes and would sit at the table with the actors, hanging on their every word. The actors made her laugh and she no longer went upstairs with anyone. They recited passages from plays by Guimerà, Pitarra and Rusiñol in the style of the most famous performers of the day. One night, Ganymede – an old, droopy-eyed, anaemic actor – dressed Biel up as a pirate and taught him, word for word, Saïd's famous monologue from *Mar i cel*.'

'Which monologue is that?' I asked, half asleep, not quite knowing how to tell Iris that the story didn't interest me.

'Wait,' she said, springing to life. 'Let me see if I can find it on the shelf with the other plays.'

She returned with a surprisingly slim book, stretched out again on the bed and began flicking through the pages until she found the passage she was looking for.

'It goes like this. Listen:

> *Honour and God's name fore'r on their lips,*
> *upon which they stamp with every step.*
> *Vile! Infidel! My sons, observe him well:*
> *he's of the same taifa as those brutes who,*
> *hypocrites speaking of brotherly love,*
> *bled us dry: not even in the stables*
> *next to the beasts did they give us shelter*
> *and, like repulsive lepers, cast us out*
> *into the hands of fate, denying us*
> *even a grave where might we rest in peace.'*

'Wow,' I said. 'That sure sounds old…'

'Let me tell the story,' said Iris, slightly annoyed.

'The image of Saïd, the pirate – who banished Morisco who betrays his desire for revenge out of love for a Christian woman – filled Biel's nights with fantastic adventures. Ganymede told Biel that actors were ordinary people like everyone else but, if they had the *crac*, they were capable of transforming into kings when they trod the boards. The greatest skill of all, however, was being able to turn even the most inadequate of spaces into a stage. And that, he added, could only be done by those who had the *crac*. Biel wanted to know what it was exactly and the aging actor replied: "It's the emotion that makes the bare words shine. Few can do it."

'The actors showed Biel how to dress up, whether as a pirate or a Christian knight, and one evening, when his mother was feeling particularly merry, they even put her shoes on him, the ones with the golden heels and silver trim, and turned him into Ophelia. His mother closed the tavern much earlier than before and she no longer entertained the priest or the flute-playing shepherd, so you can quit thinking this is some rural drama I'm telling you. She'd caress her long necklace while listening to the actors. When they asked who'd given it to her, she'd merely shrug her shoulders and bat her eyelashes, making them cheer loudly. Then her son – by now ten years old – would put on the colonel's kepi and ask her for the honour of a dance.

'Biel avidly followed all the plays the actors performed in town, but the *fin de siècle* and contemporary comedies bored him. He much preferred the tragedies, with their magnificent costumes and sublime performances. He also found Senyor Esteve a dull character and far too familiar to be of interest. In that small city of his there was any number of shopkeepers who were near carbon copies of Rusiñol's merchant protagonist. Nor did Guimerà's Manelic move him much; if anything, he reminded him of the flute-playing shepherd, the one who made his mother come downstairs in her sandals so sullen and unsociable. He never did get to see *Mar i cel*, so he never found out how Saïd's verses sounded when recited by an actor who had the *crac*.

'When war broke out, the actors disappeared. When they began to conscript seventeen year olds, his mother's first thought was to hide him in the straw loft – the same place she'd had the priest holed up, though it did nothing to save his neck – but they soon found him and, after fifteen days in a Barcelona barracks, they packed him off to where the biggest battle was raging, near Ascó, on the banks of the Ebro. I'll save you the details of the front line. After all, what do we women know about war? All I'll say is he spent months on a muddy hillside, adrift in a sea of abandoned vineyards, clambering up and sliding down, depending on how the enemy advanced, and who was now in control of the surrounding hills. He and the rest of his unit of shock troops dragged themselves along like lizards, falling here, getting up there, dying of cold and hunger, never entirely sure who was giving the orders. Sometimes a group of them would huddle together in a trench and play cards. Biel wasn't one to reminisce, but he did think about the language of his mother's shoes and the actors' verses. He was far too young, however, to be nostalgic.

'One frostbitten morning, an officer arrived on horseback and barked at them that vacations were over, that: "this ain't no holiday camp". He also informed them the enemy had tanks – and lots of them – and that they'd have to blow them up with hand grenades. "If you don't," he said, "I'll shoot the lot of you." And no prizes for guessing that one evening the enemy turned up with their tanks, but they didn't blow them up with hand grenades. Half of them died without a whimper while the other half ran away, having soiled themselves first.'

'You're imagining that.'

'It's not difficult: I grew up reading the *Hazañas bélicas* war comics.'

'Me too and that's how I know you're making all that stuff up about the Battle of the Ebro. I mean, you're just repeating all those stories about Germans and Americans. With illustrations by Boixcar, naturally.'

'The Japanese were always the villains. I don't know if it was merely because of the colour of their skin. The Germans, it depended. The Americans were always the good guys.'

'There was always that same story of the American and the German who meet in a forest, desperate, starving and alone, their faces covered in mud. Then they become friends and say things like: "first and foremost, we are human beings."'

'Yes, I remember.'

'We've spent half our lives reading these stories, stories about heroic friendships between men, just like in the westerns.'

'Of course.'

'And that's why, now, all you can do is repeat the same story. No doubt Biel gets lost on the hilltops of the Serra de Cavalls and that's where he meets the colonel, the one who gave him the hat and medal, and he says to him: "My son! Here I am: your father!

And we're on opposing sides!"'

'No, he never met the colonel again. I already told you, at the beginning, that he left for Africa, remember?'

'What difference does it make? You're only making this story up so I can get to sleep.'

'I'm not making it up.'

'Prove it.'

'I will, if you let me finish…'

'Then a ferocious battle began, brutal beyond belief. The tanks advanced. The hero of our story threw down his rifle and hid in a trench half covered by soil and stone, wishing the ground would swallow him up, his trousers wet through. He hid his head in the mud and debris and prepared himself to wait it out. He wasn't angry, or resentful, just fed up with the whole adventure. Experts in warfare say this is the worst attitude to take into battle. He heard the hum of a passing plane and prayed it was one of theirs. It was. But it flew straight over him; it must've been one of those reconnaissance planes that assess the damage and then head back to those in charge and fill them in. Above him came high-pitched whistles and explosions. According to the length of the whistle, he could tell if the projectile would fall nearby or not. To pass the time he played at measuring the distance according to the sound each projectile made. But he soon got bored. Then, there was silence. A long, terrible silence. It took him hours to even raise his head; he didn't dare to. The whole time he thought, as long as I keep my head down, they won't see me. Who knows how long he stayed like that. But the silence went on, heavy and dense. That's when he began to wonder whether he was dead already and just didn't know it.'

'They say that happens a lot in war.'

'In the end,' Iris continued, ignoring my comment, 'after hours and hours with his head hidden like that, he decided to move, first his arms, then his neck and finally his legs. Everything was in one piece. Now he knew he was alive because he was freezing to death. He raised his head and looked around. And that was when he saw him.'

'Who? Who did he see?'

'The Moor. He was sprawled out next to him, his stomach ripped apart, his jaw hanging down, and his eyes wide open. Biel barely breathed. He edged closer and the Moor moved slightly. Biel was terrified but he soon realised the Moor was long dead and if the corpse had moved it was because he'd caused some of the soil to fall away. That was when he began to weigh up his options. It was clear enough the other side had won the battle. Soon they'd be upon him and if they found him they wouldn't think twice about putting a bullet in the back of his head. He decided to put on the Moor's uniform and keep a lookout until they arrived. The short time he lay there dressed as a Moor felt eternal.'

'Those who speak of war always say the same: that time is measured differently on the battlefield.'

'During that whole time,' said Iris, 'there wasn't a single sound, until finally he heard horses' hooves and the thud of approaching footsteps. He buried his head in his arms but someone lifted it with the butt of their rifle. He was from the same side! And a colonel, no less! He then realised that the time he'd been waiting had made him a man. He stood up, leant close to the colonel, and whispered: "My name is Saïd."'

'But luck wasn't on young Biel's side. This particular Republican colonel had never seen Guimerà's play. He was from a small village in La Rioja and he merely assumed Biel was a spy pretending to be mad by saying a load of strange words that made no sense. He couldn't make head or tail of Biel's ramblings. He took him to where his regiment was camped, on the other side of the river. In a Romanesque hermitage with whitewashed walls and lit by gas lamps, they rushed through a court martial. In those days, all courts martial had an air of urgency. Why had he dressed up as a Moor? If he was a Republican soldier, as

27

he claimed, he should have trusted in victory. He should have fought to the end like his officer, whose body now lies next to a smouldering tank. Verdict: he was either a spy or a defeatist. No one considered the fact that when you're seventeen some things are difficult to explain.

'They shot him at dawn. Before the first bullet rang out, he contemplated the scene and the shadows cast by the firing squad, shadows tinged with pink, scarcely perceptible in the first light. Then, with a sudden outpouring of emotion, he began to recite Saïd's verses:

> *"and, like repulsive lepers, cast us out*
> *into the hands of fate, denying us*
> *even a grave where we might rest in peace."'*

'The soldiers didn't applaud. Nor did he have time to find out if he'd received the gift of the *crac*. He fell in the very moment he felt most full of life.

'My grandfather told me this story without my father ever knowing. He'd managed to return safe and sound from the war, but father, who owned a grocery store in our small city, always told him to keep quiet as soon as he so much as mentioned the subject. He told it to me in the vineyards, among the glistening leaves, far from the house.'

'Now, get some sleep,' said Iris. 'All of that happened a long time ago and hardly anyone remembers it now.'

I'm not sure if Iris really made that last remark or not, but what I can say is that a deep sleep swept over me, for there are stories so old that they become like lullabies in times of peace.

That's why I'm telling it to you now. *You who live free from war and wave.*

MAR

To Montserrat Blanes

Life has taught me to think but thinking has not taught me to live.
HERZEN

I

It has been two years since Mar went her own way. Two years since the day her Citroën Mehari disappeared on the Toses mountain pass, vanished off the face of the earth, as they say. She was pulled from the wreckage and rushed to hospital where I stood, staring at the tubes sticking out of her, thinking my God, what a mess, although I was too embarrassed to breathe a word of it to Ferran.

Two years since the day I saw her through the glass, her head shaved, staring back at me but no longer seeing because she was already far away, God knows where, but far enough not to be able to laugh at my feminist theories or to scream at me that children don't belong to anybody. Two years I've been living in a freeze frame, convinced the woman I was by her side was nothing but a lie that she helped me to create, an illusion, and that her way of life had to end like that: tubes sticking out of her, head shaved and breathing, because that is what the men in white wanted, men who knew nothing of us. What could they know? Even if they had known anything they would only have said what everyone else did, that we 'got along,' because the word to describe what was born the day I first laid eyes on her – was it on the train? Or before with Miss Moneypenny? – has yet to be written. Nor was I ever able to come up with one despite, in those days, devouring every book on feminism I could lay my hands on.

But, then again, it never once occurred to me to give a name to that period of silence, madness and noise, to those moments when the hours would melt into timelessness and our intellectual friends, while watching us, would frown or raise an eyebrow. 'They've got some nerve,' said their suspicious eyes while they stared, unaware of their own fear. 'Oh, they've got some nerve alright, always down at the beach, hugging, kissing, running and laughing, saying silly things and gazing at one other.' The whole lot of them, thick pencils at the ready, desperate to define the indefinable. 'Those two get along, they're two peas in a pod, there's definitely something going on between them.' Their eyes said all of that, yet perhaps with an even more limited vocabulary because, as Mar always told me, they couldn't comprehend that we loved in a different way, without going to bed with one another, without 'screwing', as they no doubt would have put it. We made love when we held hands and lost ourselves in the contemplation of the sea, sat in the wet sand, the water lapping against our feet, having completely lost track of time, while the kids ran free along the beach. Before Ernest took them away, of course. We would focus on our own personal silences which, on occasion, searched for the other's and at times sought distance, as only the silence between two people capable of conversing without words can ever be, without scripts, without the need to explain how they feel or what they perceive, just looking out to sea and thinking how we'd come to share the same body or were, in fact, bodiless, or perhaps had two separate bodies that had found one another after floating like fools through an unknown, distant galaxy.

Two years have gone by and she might not even recognise me anymore. I've gone back to being smart and sensible, to reading books to explain what I don't understand. Thinking about it now, the time we spent together was too brief, far too brief for me to keep on as though Mar were still here. She left without warning. Surplus to requirements, she went back to her universe, only I couldn't go with her. And who knows? Upon seeing similar cases to ours, maybe I also stare suspiciously, unaware of my fear, speak with a limited vocabulary and frown or raise an eyebrow. I felt something die in me, not when I saw her lying there with tubes sticking out of her, her head shaved, but afterwards because this sort of certainty never comes until later, when there is nothing you can do about it anymore. Perhaps it arrived the day Ferran and I separated, when I let everything crash and burn without ever having said how much I loved him, when all I wanted was to catch a high-speed train and yet, at the same time, remain fixed to the ground, to flee and to remain, to transform everything and for it all to stay the same. In short, to see things differently and to go back to how I saw things before I first laid eyes on Mar.

I remember a discussion which later gained legendary status between the two of us: a discussion about round tables and circumferences. It still tickles me just thinking about how Ferran tried to get Mar to understand that the edge of a round table is, in fact, called the circumference implying, therefore, a constant confluence of its lateral points at the table's geometrical centre, and Mar made him repeat it, goodness knows how many times, just to observe the serious look on his face and his need to explain everything scientifically, even if it was just a stupid round table.

I stood there for a long while watching the gentle cadence of her body controlled by the respirator, a body forced to continue breathing, up and down, up and down, while she was already far away. I had two contrasting, yet almost simultaneous, reactions. One was to rebel against the machine and science, allied in their desire to keep her alive when she'd already decided to leave; the other was to be wildly angry with her because it was as though I'd also stopped breathing, as if I too had tubes sticking out of me, my head shaved, and a machine forcing my chest to move up and down, angry because I'd have to go back to 'faking it', as they say, to pretending I was someone I wasn't, making it look as though my separation from Ferran were just a small stop on this damn thing we call life, forced to live a thousand lives again: affectionate mother without a guilt complex; hysterical mother with all the hang-ups in the world; intellectual giving talks on women's liberation; female who knows, at least theoretically, how to satisfy her male lover; and friend and confident to women who also felt like failures yet had the courage to admit it, something I could never do in a million years. And all because Mar had decided to go her own way.

Two years since the day with the respirator and the tubes, and three since I first saw her. I can still picture it as vividly in my mind as I could throughout the entire year we were together. It was Mar who always got it mixed up, not me. We were on the train and suddenly she started talking to me as if we'd known each other for years. It was only later that I realised she always spoke like that to strangers – the ones she got 'good vibes' from, of course. She liked to repeat to me that people either loved one another or they didn't: 'People either love one another or they don't. And that's all there is to it,' she'd say, switching from Catalan to Castilian to do so. I eventually found out she'd pinched the line from Shirley MacLaine, who says the same thing in *The Apartment*, only Shirley does it with teary eyes staining her cheeks with mascara. When I called her out, she merely said: 'So what? Films haven't invented anything new. They just suck up the words already floating in the air.'

The first time she spoke to me I was in the middle of a discussion with my sister about Ferran, who was shopping around for an inexpensive but reliable 4 x 4. Mar offered her two cents on the subject just as we were agreeing that the Citroën Dyane was likely a better option than the Renault 4. I remember it as if it were yesterday; she said what Ferran should really do is get himself a Citroën 2CV, the only drawback being the oil. She got straight to the point, without any introductions, and when she was finished she didn't say another word, but just went back to looking out of the window as though not having said a thing.

Naturally, I was taken aback because it was unthinkable to me for a complete stranger to comment on a private conversation and, what's more, in such a manner, as if it were the most normal thing in the world. 'What a rude woman,' I muttered to myself, because hardwired into my psyche is the precept that sticking one's nose in where it's not wanted is the height of bad taste. But she simply said that about the 2CV and the oil, and then kept quiet, as though the dusty, tired landscape of the Barcelona suburbs had suddenly captivated her. She had drifted away, lost in her own thoughts, certain she'd said just the right amount.

I couldn't take my eyes off her. I was sure I'd seen her someplace before but I couldn't think where. I even mentioned it to my sister. Her face reminded me of all those Romanesque woodcarvings, originally adorned with bright colours, on display in the tiny chapels dotted across the Pyrenees, with their sharp features, narrow jaws and thin noses. But there was also something of the wild animal mixed in with it which clashed with my mental image of Romanesque sculptures and their stoical faces accustomed to the harsh winter weather and perilous mountain passes. Maybe it was on account of her hair, which was as blonde as a barley field in summer and made me think of an androgynous Renaissance page with olive skin and small eyes, like a weasel in the forest at night. When I revealed this to her later on she told me that I classified things instead of seeing them, that I only got excited before beauty or mystery if I was expecting to be excited by it. I prepared myself too much, she said, as if, before tasting excitement, I had to rehearse it first. Now that she's dead, I can say – with or without impunity, I really don't know – that her eyes didn't seem of this world. But then we tend to say that about a dead person, especially when we see them in a photograph.

Perhaps I was attracted by what I perceived in her as innocence but which was, in fact, a merry immorality. She unearthed feelings I didn't care to define but which had long been lurking deep inside of me, as dark as the thoughts I didn't dare express, feelings I wasn't prepared to show to anyone, even less so in front of Ferran. I gave people exactly what they wanted from me – one of the keys to success, as we all know – which, in my case, meant sound judgement at conferences, a clear diagnosis on the pitfalls of contemporary women, and all that stuff about spiders' webs, ownership and how we've been belittled since birth. She would be waiting for me after each talk but she never said a word, not even if I'd been fantastic or a fantastic bore, nothing. She'd be sitting in her beat up Mehari, which would cough into action as she started the engine, and then whisk me far away, perhaps to gaze out to sea from one of our favourite beaches, surrounded by empty Coca-Cola bottles, rusty tools and old, discarded espadrilles. We hardly said a word, we certainly didn't reinvent anything, but it was only with her that I lost my fear, the fear of revealing who I believe myself to be, that little girl I keep hidden in the deep, damp depths of my inner self.

I quickly began to admire her, for I'm incapable of loving someone I don't admire – something of which she was unaware, but my admiration for her obeyed the norms I had immediately to hand, that is, as though I were a man and she the mysterious woman all men are looking for, that raw material, that piece of pure, unadulterated nature. When I was with her I forgot about books, theories, logic, sense and all the intellectualisms that had convinced me I was far better off living alone, constrained by a narrow circle of introspection, renouncing my impulses and desires, and respecting the rules of my role as the *femme savant*: the woman from whom everyone expects an illuminating answer.

I was making a mistake but I didn't know how to go about it any other way. I didn't know how to love like she did. I had to put a price on everything. If I give you '*x*' today, you can expect a bill for the same tomorrow. *Quid pro quo.* But she gave herself without precaution and that was precisely what I fell in love with. She didn't allow herself to be dominated, not because she wanted to rebel but because she had no desire to dominate anyone herself. She wasn't emancipating herself from any master for the simple reason that she didn't belong to anybody. Her attitude had nothing to do with the deliberate demeanour of the liberated, anti-bourgeois woman and quite possibly my love was born out of jealousy – because sometimes love is mothered by envy –, the jealousy of knowing I'd never be like her. Soon enough I began thinking she'd arrived from another galaxy because I simply couldn't compute how she was capable of living purely for the day, without the need for projects or theories or reflecting on the repression of our childhoods and how we've been cheated from day one. Instead, she'd always say how happy she had been as a child and, in doing so, effortlessly put into practice the theories of so-called enlightened women like me whose fear and resentment had prevented from attaining liberation once and for all. She laughed out loud when I told her she was a feminist without realising it and she poked fun at me when I confessed to her how much I admired intelligence and culture in people and that that was what had attracted me so much to Ferran. 'Oh,' she replied with faux naivety, 'so you mean you're not with Ferran because you're afraid?' She didn't say what I was afraid of, but we both knew exactly what she was talking about.

II

She awoke in me what has only been vaguely, and quite crudely, defined as a supernatural yet telluric force: something women have delighted in describing as the lost, silent nexus of our grandmothers and great grandmothers who buried their complaints and sealed off their pleasures behind immense, isolating walls. I only became aware of it when I saw her lying in the hospital bed with tubes sticking out of her, an inert body being forced to breathe by scientific progress. God, how I despised her. I despised that passive body offering no resistance. I despised it because it had no memory of having once been happy.

When I stepped off the train, it hit me. Of course I knew who the girl with the olive skin was! I began to compose an image in my mind of an exact location, finally placing her in the village square in the hills above Barcelona where we lived. She was the one I saw revealing her backside as she bent over to do up her children's coats before they got on the school bus. She was wearing an horrendous pair of orange knee-high boots and a leather miniskirt. I remember the whispering voice saying: 'Look at her, that one in the orange boots, she's shameless.' And I saw someone next to me pointing an accusatory forefinger. 'A shameless tramp,' repeated the voice. 'She lives with her husband and her lover, all three of them shacked up under one roof.' I turned towards the person who had uttered those slurs and saw it was Miss Moneypenny. With as much dignity as I could muster, I informed her that I wasn't the least bit interested in such stories. I was lying, of course. But I was so immersed in my role as the discreet, rational intellectual that I was blind to the fact it was nothing but a reflection of the hypocrisies and conventions of the neighbourhood I'd grown up in. It came as no surprise when I learnt, much later, that Miss Moneypenny thought I was stuck-up. My dignified response had nothing to do with rationality or discretion but with my class instinct, which obliged me to give a wide berth to women like Miss Moneypenny. I could defend a woman considered a shameless tramp who lived with her husband and her lover, all three of them shacked up under one roof, but by no means could I be caught cutting a woman guided by the rules of the rumour mill any slack. Ferran and I had decided to live in that sweaty, secluded village among the most marginalised in society – the *Lumpenproletariat* – as a literal interpretation of our socialist ideals but, as we would later discover, our ideals only existed in our heads.

What I was yet to learn, however, was that there is a barrier beyond that of money and ideals: namely, language. Miss Moneypenny's indiscreet, idle talk was her way of modelling the raw material in her life, and that material was nothing less than what other people did and said. Writers are no different, though they like to believe they do it better. Intellectuals turn up announcing that gossip is culture and a deft way of sticking one's nose in where it isn't invited yet, in doing so, they act no differently from Miss Moneypenny, only they season it with sweeping statements and a few teaspoons of transcendence. What's more, they get paid handsomely to do what she happily did for free. No doubt this was why Ferran and I ended up leaving the hot, humid village on the hill because there was no way of reconciling our ideals with people like Miss Moneypenny, who oscillated so carelessly between charity and cruelty without ever stopping to consider their motives. But Mar was on friendly terms with her and she knew perfectly well that she called her a shameless tramp behind her back but she also knew that she was desperately unhappy, unhappy because she was only twenty-one and had just fallen pregnant for a third time with Mr Moneypenny, a man who enjoyed playing the big shot, a flashy type who earned a 'few bob' doing piecework and spent half his wages in the square on a Saturday buying everyone drinks. Mar also knew she was slowly wasting away with weariness and remorse, wiping bums and noses all day, and lounging on the three-piece suite, surrounded by flowery wallpaper and a couple of brats who don't stop bawling for a second. It took me a long time to twig that the only diversion left to Miss Moneypenny was being able to tell me that Mar was a shameless tramp who lived with her husband and her lover, all three of them shacked up under one roof.

At first glance, Mar seemed like a cross between a rich kid and a waitress in a strip club. She was always the centre of attention but retained the special ability to vanish from view with the vaguest of valedictions that only the rich can pull off, the ones who have been prepped and polished to the point that no one even notices. I soon saw how she incited a sensual response from everyone, both adults and children alike. She was amoral without being aware of it. Perhaps that's why my girlfriends resented her and called her a 'vamp'. She gave the impression of having imbibed everything without the slightest effort or hint of inner turmoil. Each time she gave herself to a man, she did so fully, and the following day she went back to loving with the same life force as ever. She never hid what she felt. 'She's too female,' Ferran used to say to me, but all I could do was repeat that, having no desire to possess or be possessed, she was the only person I knew who was oblivious to jealousy.

After the conversation with Miss Moneypenny, when I earned the reputation of being stuck-up, I forgot all about her. Then came the day on the train when she stuck her oar into our conversation to mention that about the 2CV and the oil. Now I realise that our relationship was built upon movement: it began on the train and ended the night of the accident, the night she left in her beat up Mehari. Our relationship was a series of concentric circles, a spiral that thrust us ever onwards as we threw caution to the wind. She never interfered in my relationship with Ferran, but they were poles apart. My relationship with Ferran was static, still, and he couldn't stand our agitation, our incessant movement towards a distant point that continually beckoned us. For Ferran, that was what madness looked like. But contained within our movement was too much desire to live for it ever to be madness.

I placed her as I climbed the stairs from the railway platform: the girl with the olive skin was the shameless tramp from the village. With time, I ended up calling her my 'super tramp' or my 'slut', and each time I did my mouth filled with a bittersweet taste because I'd go back to being that little girl who had learnt to break the rules through language. When I told her what Miss Moneypenny said about her I was worried she'd get angry but instead she roared with laughter: 'Ha, ha, ha! So, I'm the village bike!' but then she fell silent before whispering, as if all of a sudden she'd cottoned on: 'Perhaps I *am* a slut.' She repeated the word once, twice, a hundred times: 'Slut, slut, slut… we're just a couple of sluts.' That was the only conclusion she drew from it. 'Sure, but I mean, you're more of a slut than I am,' I replied. 'Oh, of course,' she fired back, 'because *you* present yourself as a smart-arse intellectual. In other words, you're a hypocrite.' I asked her why the attitude all the time towards intellectuals, and she immediately stopped laughing, abandoned her jocular tone and said: 'Because you're always trying to demonstrate what other people experience, as if you were all stone dead or something. You're obsessed with explaining everything, as though chance and fate were for ordinary people without any common sense.' 'Okay, okay,' I conceded gracefully, 'I'm a slut on the inside and you're a slut on the outside, deal?' While she preferred to let the whole thing slide, I continued: 'You know, when I was fifteen I used to go red like a tomato when someone said slut and when I was thirteen I once ran as if I'd seen a ghost when I saw it scrawled on a wall in chalk.' I said the word slowly, savouring its sound: I'm a slut, a *s-lu-t*.' I'd never have dreamt of saying that word in front of Ferran; perhaps 'prostitute' or, in a more ironic tone, 'strumpet', which I'd rhyme with 'jazz trumpet' or 'English crumpet', but then there is nothing transgressive about sarcasm. With Nana I'd likely have said a 'you-know-what', 'a working girl' or *cocotte*; a word that always made me think of Paris during the *Belle Époque* and the oyster restaurants on Place Pigalle.

I don't remember how or when our paths crossed again. Perhaps it was on one of those endless evenings when everything felt monotonous and I was waiting for Ferran to return home with a prolonged inner yawn. I seem to recall us bumping into one another at the bus stop and sussing one another out with furtive glances before our boys came bundling towards us and began tugging on our sleeves. We must have looked like a couple of canines trying to catch each other's scent. Nor do I remember who led who up the steep muddy path, like it was nothing, but what I do know is that, having exchanged just a couple of remarks, I found myself sitting in the passenger seat of her Mehari. For my two, it was the height of entertainment. It was already getting dark as we began driving up to the forest, in reality a meagre copse with dry, diseased pines surrounded by clusters of bushes and piles of rubbish. She drove without haste or fear, her gaze fixed on some distant point and her left hand gripping the door whenever it threatened to swing open. Mine had been secured with a piece of rope. She drove calmly but also with the air of someone fleeing. Despite being left slightly disorientated by the constant jolting and swaying, I was able to observe her out of the corner of my eye and make out, amid the shadows, a tense face that emitted a mysterious, magical force. Perhaps it was on account of how her skin would go abruptly from black to indigo and back to black again, but it seemed a hard, aggressive face. Or possibly it was because of her firm jaw and her eyes lost on some distant point, a point I couldn't reach because all I perceived were the languishing pines coated in the grey dust blowing up from Barcelona. Later I realised that her car transformed her; her body became more supple and she acquired a potency and poise that otherwise went undetected. Danger made her invulnerable.

One day she came right out and said it: 'You know something? This is how I'd like to die: looking straight ahead.' I clung on the best I could with each swerve while everything jolted inside the car. In the back, the boys rolled around like ragdolls, shouting that we were on a jungle safari, and all we could hear was their joyous racket and the clanging of tools. The seats jigged frantically and the plastic around the windows convulsed with each bump, as though the elements had begun a frenzied dance in the forest amid the first shadows of night. I observed her profile in the half-shadow. It appeared to emerge from the night, or the dark ocean, and I thought how she was like Calypso leaving behind her lonely island to meet me. Maybe I only thought that afterwards. The only thing I do know is that I didn't breathe a word of it to Ferran.

We sat down on the grass near the hilltop café bar. A period of patchy silence and partial phrases inched along while the dying day dropped a fiery blanket over the valley. I didn't need long to know everything there was to know about her and she began telling me about her childhood memories, the sweet scent of mandarins, the kisses given to her by her father, a man she saw go from rich industrialist to shuffling vagabond. In a way, her memories were similar to mine, yet they seemed so much more exotic. I listened to how she fell madly in love with her best friend's father, a 'gorgeous' engineer who built tunnels and carriageways. All that was missing was her dubbing him a 'silver fox' and we'd have had the same clichéd character we'd been exposed to by all the countless radio serials along our pathway to adulthood. She also told me how she lost her virtue – that's right, 'her virtue' – inside a tunnel used to test jet engines.

She recounted it all without once modulating her voice, as if reciting a litany, the result being that there was nothing theatrical about her industrialist father who ended up homeless or her seduction in a tunnel surrounded, not by the sweet scent of mandarins, but the stench of tar and petrol and the sound of engines buzzing like a violent swarm of bees. And she was equally as serious when, later on, she told me about Ernest, her cowardly, God-fearing cousin, who almost went completely out of his mind over an uncle on her mother's side, a 'big time Charlie' and a 'merry Andrew' – yes, that is what she really called him – who 'popped his cork and then his clogs' in a cathouse, after an attack of angina. Well, what she actually said was apoplexy, if I'm not mistaken. Then she went straight into explaining how her family forced her to marry this cowardly, God-fearing cousin of hers after finding out about her deflowering in a tunnel at the hands of a handsome engineer who also just happened to be her best friend's father.

Yet, much more than her monotonous voice and the colourful content of those tales far too unreal to be written about, what I remember most of all was the nonchalance with which she told me them, sucking the whole time on her tonic water with a pink straw. Not just the image of the straw but also the fragrance of the pine trees, her lunar profile and the way she told me some of the strangest stories I'd ever heard, as if they were the most normal things in the world. Like, for example, her husband's delusion that if he did it with her – yes, she really did say 'it' – he'd end up going the same way as dear uncle Claudi, the name of the 'big time Charlie', 'merry Andrew' of an uncle who had sown the honourable family loam with the seeds of scorn and shame. She told me about the range of revealing night dresses she'd bought to do 'it', because her husband's horror was incomprehensible to her. But soon she realised there was absolutely no way of persuading him because he was convinced that under no circumstances whatsoever could they do 'it'. At night he would lie in bed with the blanket pulled up to his chin and shout that she was a murderer.

She stopped to scratch her cheek with the pink straw before painting an image of how she would slink through the darkness towards that trembling body hiding under the apple green cover, wearing nothing but a skimpy silk dress, slowly revealing one thigh, then the other, just as she'd seen in the movies because, you see, it never entered her head that Ernest – her husband and cousin – could be such a hopeless case. Nevertheless, accepting that curing him was beyond her reach, she eventually went to visit her husband-cousin's spiritual father, a smooth-talking Jesuit who in his younger days had been quite the celebrity. He consoled her before initiating an – unsuccessful – attempt to seduce her, something she only became aware of much later after her husband had already been cured by a renowned psychoanalyst just one or two years younger than the priest.

I don't know why I'm flooding my mind with these memories, all of them so muddled and mixed up. Maybe because today it's two years since she went her own way and almost three since the day she sucked her tonic water through a pink straw surrounded by the scent of pine, her lunar profile outlined by the warm light of a fiery evening sky. She told me that, thanks to the psychoanalyst, her husband overcame his phobia of dying during intercourse but that, by then, she'd lost the desire to make love to him and there was no way of getting it back. She told the story as though it were no big deal, as if the protagonist were a stranger, a character from a cheap novel so bad and of such little consequence that it wasn't worth worrying about. And perhaps that is what surprised me most of all: not the whole story in itself, or her husband's night terrors, or the charismatic priest's wandering eyes, but her way of telling it, free from histrionics, an ancient custom that, it seemed to me, women have lost without being aware of it.

We hardly said a word on the way home. The boys, happy and covered in sweat, were dozing on the backseat and the only sound was that of the tools clanging as they struck one another. She dropped us off in front of the house and I offered for her to come in and meet Ferran, despite knowing his reaction would undoubtedly be to close his eyes, shrug, and merely take Mar as my latest discovery. Neither he nor I could have known, however, that the undefinable thing we'd given life to that day was destined to die less than a year from then.

I do wonder whether Mar's shining virtue was having turned up at the right time, just as a part of me was also dying. Similarly, I question if I wasn't, in fact, searching for the balance between time and space we only ever achieve when we're young and self-centred, a balance I hadn't had time to strike with Ferran. I was far too concerned with forming the paradigm of the intellectual couple dedicated to literature but, in reality, we were isolated from the stories of others, our marital life was meaningless, and we took a perverse pride in having no time to love or to probe beyond the limits of the immense affection we purported to have for all humanity. It wasn't long before we were watching everything shatter beyond repair. When Ferran finally left home, it didn't make me any more nostalgic for Mar because his departure left its own void. It was Mar who showed me how our collective notion, that one romance can substitute another, was fatuous and puerile. She didn't put it quite like that, of course, because Mar never hypothesised in such a way; she lived and left us, and people like us, to do the theorising.

Maybe that is why I refused to recognise the defenceless body exhibited on the other side of the polished glass, forced to breathe artificially. I didn't want to have to say goodbye to a gaping mouth, a pair of blind eyes and two lifeless hands flopped at her side. I didn't want to bid farewell to a ragdoll wired up to tubes and machines in an intensive care unit. Regardless of the respirator's infallible marking of every beat and breath, she had decided that she couldn't go on living among us and to instead go her own way. Perhaps I also resented her because she was condemning me to a return to thinking about life rather than living it. She kindled the beginnings of a new woman in me, something no man had been capable of doing, but these shoots of a new beginning had already withered and died. When I introduced her to Ferran both of them just stood there, awkward and lost for words, until Mar tried to pick up the cat. Frightened, it ran away but as I went to corner it so she might stroke it a while, she calmly told me: 'Leave it be, cats only want to be loved when they need it.'

As time went by, I discovered more about her. Like, for example, her decision to go and live with the boys on her own not long after her husband was cured. He couldn't swallow the fact that she no longer slinked through the darkness in a see-through slip, not now he was over the vision of his dead uncle spread-eagled in a brothel, not now he wanted her so bad. 'Come on,' he would purr, 'come and fool around a bit.' And she'd go and fool around, but only for a bit, because she soon got fed up and was wrenching herself free of him. When Ernest finally left home, she told me he went with a terrifying look on his face, as if saying: 'Oh, you'll pay for this.' In the end, none of what Miss Moneypenny had been going around saying about Mar living with her husband and her lover, all three of them shacked up under one roof, had a shred of truth to it. My God, how we giggled when she told me her husband-cousin, just before leaving, had said he loved her so much he could kill for her, or when he said: Oh sweetheart, if only some accident would leave you paralysed so I could take care of you and wheel you about everywhere in a chair.' Mar couldn't see Ernest's saintly face beholding her through the glass or the pleasure in his soppy, ferret eyes as he stared at her inert body. It made me furious not to be able to tell Mar about it. We would have simply howled with laughter.

Afterwards came the whole bizarre business with the stake. Mar had already started to go her own way but all Ernest wanted to do, now that he was well and truly over his crisis, was to hump all day. Try as he might, however, he could never hold her down. She began to look around her as though everything had been reborn in that precise moment just for her, and she absorbed it attentively with her gaze, the gateway to the memory. She would arrive home and almost not be able to get through the door, on one occasion getting the fright of her life. Something rough had rubbed against her face and only after recovering her senses did she see her husband had nailed a string of garlic above the door. 'He thinks I'm a vampire,' she confided in me, 'He even sleeps with a wooden stake by the bed because he's convinced I'll transform into a female version of Count Dracula. You know, one of these days, he'll drive that damn thing into my heart.'

But Ernest's madness was nocturnal and thus much easier for him to convince everyone that Mar was the crazy one, a woman incapable of mothering her sons as God intended: 'I mean, just look at the boys, they eat when they feel like it, they go around with muddy shoes, their coats hanging off their arms and their trousers held up with safety pins.' Admittedly, that was all true, but it was also true when I say that I'd never seen such happy, cheeky, boisterous boys, a couple of acrobats who would caress and squeeze their mother's generous body whenever they got the urge before sprinting off to climb the tallest tree and shout down the tale of Sinbad and the Princess. But Mar didn't realise her husband was holding all the aces: his short-lived depression over the death of dear uncle Claudi had been erased from memory, and his night-time assertion that Mar was a vampire from whom he had to defend himself with a wooden stake didn't come into it because nobody would have believed such an absurd story for a second. Mar hadn't known how to prepare for what was coming or, perhaps, she merely misread the signs, because she always was unable to accept that the future is nothing but a repetition of the present, making it precisely the present that we have to hold down, to keep in check. Nor did she consider the fact that, in the eyes of the world – that is, in the eyes of custom and convention – Ernest was an honest family man and a valued employee who kept his kids clean and combed at all times. Sure, they didn't shout like before and they didn't seem half as happy but, in the eyes of the world, those were mere details.

One by one, Mar picked events apart for me as though none of it were happening to her. Not once, however, did I suspect she was preparing to set sail. Our life together reminded me of a phrase that a Galician author I admire often uses: she 'lay alongside me'. In other words, she was like a boat tethered to my side but separated by buoys which, incidentally, was exactly how I wanted to exist alongside Ferran, despite his never comprehending it. I now wonder whether Ferran left because Mar had made me desire again and he, like most people, was unable to embrace fantasy and reality in the same person. Life at home descended into mayhem, a veritable madhouse. The boys learnt to climb the tallest trees and to re-enact the story of Sinbad and the Princess, we slept all three of us in the same bed, and they constantly clamoured to go on safari with Mar's two in her Mehari, each time dustier, dirtier and dotted with more petrol stains, the doors half hanging off, torn newspapers, rusty tools, oily rags, bits of rope and empty Coca-Cola bottles everywhere. The car would leapfrog up the dusty hillside towards the dreary clearing and the dying pines with their half-rotten trunks and spindly ash-coloured branches that invited no bird to perch on them. The boys stamped their feet in the back before rolling and tumbling out the door and pulling their pants down to see which of them could wee the furthest. I thought how she was exactly like her Mehari: so terribly welcoming yet so desperately temporary. I yearned to abandon the structure holding me in place, to leave behind the conventions of the neighbourhood I'd grown up in and its rules and regulations that I've been playing out over the years, and dress like her and her boys, with bright-ly-coloured socks that never matched the shoes, faded jeans, garish, oversized t-shirts, and tattered jumpers that made them look like a family of scarecrows.

But it wouldn't have been the same. The bangles, bracelets, safety pins and patches only served to make Mar more alluring, more beautifully seditious. Her lunar profile stood out even more when she was curled up next to me on the sofa, her eyes closed as though she were already dead, listening to Chopin's Piano Concerto No.2. She didn't care for rock music, she never watched television, she hardly ever read; just hours and hours listening to Chopin as if she'd already begun to drift away. One day, her hand resting on the steering wheel, gazing directly ahead as if from a ship's prow and immersed in the pungent, decrepit beauty of the forest, she uttered: 'If I have to die, this is how I want to go.'

When I visited her house for the first time I almost didn't recognise her in the tiny photo pinned to the wall. It was of a couple. The man wore a tie, his hair carefully parted and a bright, happy smile, while his arm sat around the waist of a dumpy girl-next-door type. She had her hair backcombed into one of those hairstyles that were all the rage in the sixties and she looked a lot shorter in the photo than she was in real life. Her plump figure suggested a voluptuous future to be just around the corner. She stared back at the man protecting her with the sprightly, nimble look of the recently enamoured. And with good reason too, because the man with the protective embrace was none other than the cowardly, God-fearing cousin who welcomed her in from the cold in full view of everyone after she'd been deflowered by her best friend's father in a tunnel used to test jet engines.

III

All of that, of course, was long before Ernest's trauma over uncle Claudi's final trip to the bordello, and even longer before he began to yell: 'Murderer!' at her and suspect she was a vampire. She began avoiding the house, not because of the string of garlic above the door or the wooden stake by the bed, but because she'd already begun to go her own way. She had buried the girl with the beehive and the beginnings of a full figure a long time before and, what's more, she did it without so much as a passing glance at any of the books I've had to read, only to end up back where I started. Perhaps that's why I resented and adored her the day with the tubes; I adored her ability to change, to transform herself, yet I resented the happiness I'd experienced next to her. I've never needed any man to protect me, and I've certainly never backcombed my hair, but then neither have I ever attempted a transformation.

Each day she got home a little later. Some days it was on account of our having gone up to the dusty hilltop together but on others it was because she'd been with her Argentine, the man who taught her 'all the pleasures of a Hollywood love affair', as she put it. She was a dedicated student, despite him being ten years her junior and having his heart set on becoming a sailor. But that didn't bother her in the slightest; on the contrary, it galvanised her. She learnt to hold her gaze before the eternal plenitude of his naked body and to look at and know her own in the same way that she strived to know his, fully aware that the fusion of two bodies is an open question only on occasions eliciting an answer. In fact, she was such a devoted disciple of her seaman that she soon had no desire whatsoever to sleep with Ernest. He'd had his chance and now all he provoked in her was pity: a sapping sensation that receives nothing in return. Furthermore, Mar had begun to make comparisons and this, more than anything else, marks the beginning of the end, if not the end, of any relationship. One day, however, her Argentine – the young sailor who had taught her to revere her body through his – upped and left, perhaps because they both knew it was high time to leave that temporary harbour. She liked telling me of his sweet words that swore nothing eternal; words that were, according to her, as equally as ephemeral as those that did attempt to be everlasting.

She also revealed how she'd learnt to view herself in the mirror, to look at herself differently, not to check if a dress or a certain hairstyle suited her, and certainly not to scrutinise, with our usual masochism, the slow deterioration of skin and muscles, but to cherish her figure and how she was made, hers and hers alone, not the images we're bombarded with day in, day out in magazines and on television. She learnt to love her curves because 'they are me, just like yours are you', and she took the time to observe each part of her body, including our notorious cove, worshipped and condemned by poets, ignored by mystics, exploited by artistic obsessions, but seldom examined closely by us. The humid, generous cove, not as a symbol of chastity but the promise of an inner presence. She would pause to probe her furthest reaches and most intimate folds, sensing the minute transformations that inform us of pleasure's imminent arrival, yet always free from the fear of being conquered, for she was quick to realise that we have nothing to lose in a night of lovemaking if we know why we are giving ourselves. All this she would explain to me, sat by my side, on the dusty hilltop.

The Argentine departed, as all landlocked sailors must, but she still considered herself a novice in questions of love. And that is when Joaquim appeared on the scene. Or was he after the music teacher? I can't remember and it's sad knowing she isn't here to set me straight. Perhaps Joaquim did come first, because he was fiercely jealous of Ernest and couldn't understand why she wouldn't leave him. Mar spent a lot of nights helping out at Joaquim's bar and suddenly her life was filled with purpose: she had to help poor Joaquim, who'd never had so much as a penny to his name, a woeful existence from day one, she explained, first as a flea-bitten kid growing up in the most sordid, post-war poverty imaginable, then doing backbreaking, poorly paid jobs, always for piece rate, slumming it all over the city just to survive. She took well to helping Joaquim, a young man with a flat face who always went around with wet hair. So well, in fact, that I almost lost contact with her. But then she'd appear out of the blue with a bunch of wild flowers, perhaps as way of an apology, and curl up by my side and listen to Chopin while Ernest would be waiting – a lavish meal on the table and a string of garlic above the door – for her to come home. But she wouldn't go home; instead, she'd go to the bar and spend the night hanging pictures, painting the stairwell and sawing planks of wood to make shelves for behind the bar. She did the stuff of men not because she was aiming to emulate them or wanted to prove herself but for the simple reason that she enjoyed it. She wasn't taking revenge on anything or anyone when she revved her motorbike, or willed her clapped-out Mehari up the hill, making enough noise to raise the dead. She knew about electrics, she could fix a broken washing machine, she could even tell you why your car wouldn't start, but this world – magical in my eyes owing to my ignorance and disinclination – was child's play to her, none of which, it must be said, prevented her from being as delicate and as elegant as a stalactite. Maybe this is the reason why some women hated her and more than a few men were frightened of her.

His jealousy over Ernest most likely getting the better of him, Joaquim soon faded away. So, yes, I was right, this is where the music teacher comes in, a Swiss-Catalan who was infatuated with Mar. At first, they did nothing but stroll around arm in arm, like in the movies, butterflies fluttering in their stomachs, incapable of doing anything that didn't involve being together, while eating each other up, spying goodness knows what images of eternity, and endlessly repeating verses by Vicente Aleixandre. As Ernest left through the front door, the whole while imagining the day Mar would finally fall into his arms, paralysed from the waist down, the music teacher followed Joaquim's footsteps by creeping in through the back door. Yet, far from merely amassing lovers, Mar believed each individual had the right to their own story and the music teacher's was that he'd just discovered his sweetheart's love wasn't anywhere near as exclusive as his, a discovery that had left him 'spiritually maimed', as she told me without a hint of irony. He'd got embroiled in a love affair that was doomed from the very start, as they say, and Mar assured me that she was merely 'a small stop on his journey towards forgetting'. Undeterred, she taught him everything she'd learnt from the Argentine and perfected with Joaquim.

Mar felt nothing of what we might call 'loss' or 'rejection' when, not long after, the music teacher revealed he had fallen head over heels for a student of his, an enchanting little thing he wanted to introduce her to right away. Not only did Mar not feel rejected but she congratulated him and they kissed in a prelude to a night of lovemaking – their last. At daybreak, when they awoke, the music teacher whispered to her: 'I'll always be thankful to you, how can I ever forget you?' and she believed they were words spoken with sincerity. Softly, they made love in front of the fireplace in a goodbye that was both dispassionate and 'tinged with melancholy'.

When she mentioned it to me my first reaction was to ask if she didn't feel taken for a ride, I mean, surely it wasn't possible for her not to be hurt in some way by the hackneyed story of a man who seeks solace in the arms of an older woman and then, once he's had his fill, skips off into the sunset with some innocent little thing who will admire him for everything he'd been taught by her experienced hand. But either she didn't, or didn't want to, understand because she simply replied that she had never owned him and he had never owned her – they had travelled a short while together on a journey they would both look back on with affection. The only thing she ever demanded was that they truly loved her when they were together, that they saw her, that they didn't commit the all too common crime of mental adultery. When, she said to me, you find yourself at the centre of another being, 'that brief moment becomes eternal. Yes,' she added in agreement with herself, '*that's* what eternity looks like.' 'You won't last long talking that way and, what's more, believing it,' I replied, adding, 'that's just soap opera language dipped in intuitive feminism.' But she immediately shot back by saying that we intellectuals and artists think suffering will help us create and that unless we feel awful all the time we can't go on, but that we search for it out of cynicism and use suffering as a tool and nothing more. She almost sounded like Eugenio Montale's verses when he advises us not to flee from life for it evades us perfectly fine by itself. Well, that's how it seemed to me, anyway. But when she spoke like that I felt compelled to distance myself from her and return to the conventionality of signs and words, the only thing holding me in place.

She always kept an obstinate silence in front of my friends, especially when they started on one of their ideological discussions on the failures of our generation, at that point a fashionable topic of debate. 'It all passes her by,' they would say to me, referring to Mar, 'she's such a strange woman, so nonchalant.' But it was only because they had no way of classifying her, which was unforgivable in their eyes. Yet, rather than what she did or didn't say, it was her unpredictable behaviour that baffled them, which they classed as a constant contradiction. But the truth was that her presence messed up the carefully compiled archives in their minds. Almost from the very start I caught a fleeting look in Mar's eyes that distanced her both from me and my friends and I ask myself if she had, by then, already started to go her own way. She seldom spoke about her past anymore, as if no longer wanting to share it with anyone, and she stopped mentioning her wino father or her mother married to a needle and thread. She rarely evoked the smell of mandarins and the fragrance of them that stirred memories of a rough hand and the whites of two unrelenting eyes. She knew her father went about half drunk, collecting cardboard and newspapers during the daytime, and scavenging in bins at night like a scraggy fox. He lurked in the shadows of every alleyway and every street corner. 'My father's face,' she told me, 'it's green,' but when I asked why her father had a green face, she had already changed the subject. Now I think about it, it's possible that in all the men she loved, in each and every one of them, she was looking for some reflection of her father. But if it's true, she never breathed a word of it to me.

These two years I've desperately wanted to believe, to fool myself into believing, that she never thought of going her own way when she was with me; that she didn't think about it when we wandered hand in hand through the Gothic quarter, startling strangers and scandalising men, as my arm hung loosely around her neck and I felt the sweet adolescent taste of the forbidden once more. Or when we devilishly drank from the same wine glass in front of a dismayed waiter, before she began playing the role of a secretary involved in industrial espionage and I the part of a film producer about to have my wicked way with her.

IV

Since the publication of *Anna Karenina*, or perhaps even before, it has become customary for humanity to believe that happy people have no stories to tell, something I now know to be false, for if there are any stories really worth recounting, it's those of people who have known happiness. And that is exactly what I was next to Mar: a happy person. Those moments, despite their stillness, are far from dead: they are silent when I want, voluble when I choose, rising up in me as seemingly profitless fragments of memory united by pain or converging in joy to challenge my belief that the youth I'd regained thanks to Mar, was lost forever.

We'd imitate Esther Williams while soaking top and tail in the old rusty bathtub with dragon feet and afterwards, wrapped in the same towel, the one Mar stole from a luxury hotel while on holiday with Ernest, we'd sing: '*Amado miooooo, love me foreeeeever, and let foreeeeever, begin toniiiiight,*' just like Rita Hayworth does in *Gilda*. After applying all the creams we could find, we'd lean against the wall tiles and, smoking from the same long cigarette holder, imitate the dialogue from Ingmar Bergman films, which we made as boring and longwinded as possible, peppering our lines with pauses, sighs and metaphysical digressions, while staring straight ahead, not once looking at each other. Or we'd start a conversation along the lines of:

'*Oh, darling, have I mentioned that you look ravishing today?*'
'*Why no, you haven't!*'
'*I must have forgotten… That's an exquisite dress you're wearing.*'
'*Do you like it?*'
'*I dare say I prefer what you've got hidden underneath.*'
'*Oh, you rascal!*' she'd gasp before batting her eyelashes in the style of Greta Garbo.
'*And your skin! It's so soft, like a damsel's,*' I'd reply, lightly brushing a fingertip over her bare arm, while she'd pretend to shiver with excitement.
'*Oh, weally, you pwomise? But I'm all gwown up.*'
'*You're special, don't you see? You're so different to all the rest. I wish I was twenty and could start all over again! Just you and me, together, forever. But, alas, I found you too late.*'
'*Listen, sunshine, you coming up or wot? I've got a bo'le of*

bubbly with our name on it.'

'*God, you're wonderful. One can talk to a sophisticated, intelligent woman like you. When I'm at home, you're all I think about. At times, I'm convinced she'll find out about us. Oh, how I adore you!*'

At night we looked for fresh victims, which wasn't difficult. While waiting for the lights to change there was, more often than not, some Casanova ready to roll his window down, lean his head out and start sizing us up, imagining what we were like below the waist. When the lights turned green, our aspiring conqueror would crane his neck even further, looking us up and down with greater urgency, while we laid it on thick, shooting him suggestive looks. Just when he thought he'd hit the jackpot Mar would slam on the accelerator and start doing zigzags in front of our thwarted Don Juan while we blew him raspberries. This constituted one of the worst provocations imaginable because it was unpardonable for two women over the age of forty to play cat and mouse while mocking the rules of the game, rules that have been long established between the two herds. But we weren't out to get revenge on the men obliged to stick to the script just so they could feel that they were lovers with imagination. 'For this class of man,' Mar would say, 'the night is the only time when they can play out these sorts of fantasies.'

It was impossible to think in vindictive terms with Mar. She didn't hate men, she merely mocked the sadness of the game, the poverty of its established vocabulary and the lack of originality of its gestures. It was futile for me to continue theorising about the condition of women, to persist with my self-absorbed attempts to loosen the cultural and historical knot that only served to distance us from men, to go on talking to the women in the village about our castration being the basis of our resentment, all of it pointless, because this deluge of words and ideas didn't help me in the slightest. I still needed pills to sleep at night and I still cried every morning in the shower because I felt abandoned by Ferran, like some ten-a-penny protagonist out of a trashy romance novel. Mar, on the other hand, wouldn't have felt the least bit embarrassed speaking like all the protagonists that have ever appeared in all the trashy romance novels ever written. She did her own thing and she did it with a smile. And that is how things were until Mar received a letter from Ernest's lawyer. She had always been the stronger of the two but the bad blood over the boys knocked her for six. She couldn't fathom how her ex-husband – the cousin she'd taken pity on – could treat her like an enemy.

v

Our time together was too brief, far too brief for me to fully comprehend that a different way of life was possible, that it really was within my grasp. It was a time when all the pieces of the jigsaw had fallen into place, as if each of my body's extremities were both separate from and joined to one another, and my mind connected to an ever-expanding universe. For that one year I wasn't just the person I am, but the person I believe I have the potential to be. And it wasn't because of the games we played, or how we laughed, or the affection we showed. Nor was it because of our secret sense of triumph each time men shouted: 'Dykes!' at us on the street after seeing us holding hands, a horrifying sin if you consider that two women were only permitted to link arms. Two females strolling arm in arm were, in their eyes, two 'good little girls', thus two females holding hands had to be, according to their logic, lovers. Nor was it because of how, all of a sudden, we would hug each other on the beach in full view of everyone just because we had the urge to, right there, in that very moment, or when we would go and pinch modernist flowerpots out of the front gardens of the summer houses in our village on those fresh, moonless August nights. Suddenly, Mar turned to me and said: 'Don't you see how we make love? Don't you see how two women can love one another differently? I can't explain it… I just know it's different from a man and a woman.'

I said I saw it but I didn't say a word about the terrifying fissure that was opening below my very feet. But she must have guessed as much because she later suggested we take her Mehari and head north. 'They don't understand us,' she kept repeating. And by 'they' she meant the world. And by the 'world' she meant the aggressive, anonymous masculine masses who would never forgive us our mystery, our flaunting of a still nameless connection and, above all, the fact that we didn't need them to do 'it'. In short, for sharing something destined to remain a dark, unexplored continent.

I only kissed her the one time. It was at the studio flat I rented after reading *A Room of One's Own*, a studio I had to give up a short while later, just after Mar's death, because my separation from Ferran had left me penniless and, as we all know, to have a room of one's own one needs five hundred pounds a year. We were lying on a Berber blanket, tired after so much rummaging through the bric-a-brac and junk left by the previous tenant. It was right before Ernest got himself a lawyer and informed Mar about the kids, and not long before the accident. We were discussing the old woman who had died alone in the flat, surrounded by stacks of old newspapers, and rubbish bags arranged neatly throughout the house. We found the old lady's spirit bewitching. Amid a heap of enormous patched underpants, mother of pearl rosaries, a yellowed prayer book and grey flannel shirts, we came across the old lady's letters and photographs, together with a moth-eaten fox fur. Mar wrapped it around her neck, and began strutting up and down the corridor while swaying her hips. I told her she looked like a *cocotte*.

We relived the old, unknown woman's story, a story that would end with her lying face down in the piss and vomit of her last binge. She was known in the neighbourhood as Lady Sherry. The photos revealed that she'd once had a lover because in each of them she appeared next to an elegant man who wore a white hat with a wide brim. We also discovered the man had left his wife to go and live with her when she was still a middle-aged woman with a round, chubby face. After many years together, the elegant man died without leaving a will and the old lady was left alone in the flat to wither away amid the knick-knacks and keepsakes. Soon the toilet wouldn't flush, the taps stopped working, and the filth and mountains of rubbish took over. The woman who cleaned the stairs told us that, in the end, the old lady had just enough energy to go down to the bar on the corner and knock back three or four large glasses of sherry, relishing the ancient, sweet taste on her palate. She had been left to rot, abandoned by all and sundry, and complained about by the other women in the block who, according to the cleaner, couldn't stand the stench that flowed out from her flat and filled the stairway. Amid the muck and mounds of old clothes, a few crumpled letters and photographs were the last remaining remnants of the life she had shared with the only man who had ever loved her in her whole damn life, waiting for two strangers who wanted a room of their own after reading Virginia Woolf to find them so they could appreciate the tiny, tragic gesture of a woman who left everything behind to follow a man who would end up leaving her destitute. I remember saying: 'Life isn't tragic, it's absurd. Just look at me, always going on about feminism, yet here I am getting all soppy over the corny old number of the "woman who gives it all up to run away with the man she loves"'. But Mar didn't say a thing, she just stared at the soft, at times spectral, evening light slipping through the open balcony. There was a long pause until she finally said: 'The light's beautiful.' Nothing else. Just that about the light. We were lying on the Berber blanket, her head resting on my hip, her hair tickling my stomach. And that is when I kissed her.

It has been two years since Mar went her own way, two years since the day she turned up at the studio, shaking from head to foot, telling me Ernest had seen a lawyer about taking the kids off her. Her ex-husband insisted the law was on his side and, anyway, he had cast-iron proof that she was crazy and unfit to be a mother. I told her she had to fight, that children always belong to the mother, and I can still recall, as clear as day, the fire in her eyes as she screamed: 'Children don't belong to anybody, do you understand? No one!' And that's when she suggested I went north with her. She knew there was nothing she could do, that Ernest would win custody because he had a job and money and she had nothing. She urged me to run away with her but all I wanted was for the widening rift beneath me to close once again.

She slammed the door as she left and it wasn't for another three days that I found out about the accident, about her car having plunged over the edge of the Toses mountain pass. I don't think she was running away, I think she was merely returning to a place she knew from before, a place she tried to show me here. And here is where I remain.

September, 1980 (revised September 1988)

DIVISION

That's the real distinction between people:
not between those who have secrets and those
who don't; but between those who want to
know everything and those who don't.
This search is a sign of love, I maintain.
    JULIAN BARNES, *Flaubert's Parrot*

'I hate this landscape.'

    She lay down on the blanket of dry leaves and looked up at the sky, but she didn't find the sky, merely small patches of pale light through which the sun's rays slipped surreptitiously.

    'I hate this landscape,' she repeated. 'I hate all landscapes. They're so full of literature.'

    The branches swayed softly and stretched upwards in search of warmth. Now and again she heard the deep song of a nightingale and the soft beating of wings.

> *'A different way of living.'*
> *The rambler, as he enters this place,*
> *begins to stroll at a gentler pace;*
> *he counts his steps in the silent green,*
> *stops, hears nothing, and remains unseen.*[*]

'I guess I ought to be thinking the same: how I'd like to remain unseen and for them to never find me, hidden deep under the leaves, transformed into an ant.'

    But she didn't think any of that. A tenuous ray of sun gilded the uppermost leaves of the beech trees. She listened to the silence. The poppies and sprigs swayed along the edge of the path, peppered with daisies. When Aloma was small she always made daisy chains for her.

*La fageda d'en Jordà, by Joan Maragall

'I'll make a bouquet and fill the house with wild flowers.'

She smiled. Their friends all said they had the prettiest house. They bought it when Aloma was fifteen and it took three years to fully restore. They had to completely redo the roof and remove the façade because the previous owners had plastered over the original. Conrad said the locals had lost the taste for their own architecture. They gave Aloma the bedroom overlooking the valley and fitted it with a large window. 'This way you'll get to see the mountains every morning,' her father said. She only got to see them one summer. The mountain range was also visible from the veranda, which took on silver hues at night. 'The prettiest house in the valley,' they all said. And they said it, above all, because of the wooden balconies overflowing with foliage that hung down like drapes to merge with the meadow. She put a clay vase and a bouquet in every room and, in the middle of the walnut dining table, a porcelain bowl full of fruit. She had a flair for combining colours, everyone said so. White spring grapes next to imperial purple figs, wild plums beside freshly picked peaches, and all of it resting upon small fern leaves, the ones that burst with green. She exhaled deeply, as if emptying herself of air, and stretched her arms. Then she raised her legs and felt the blood sink to her chest.

She emerged from the beech forest, walked towards to the main road and stopped by a crossroads. It wouldn't be long until the car arrived. The farmhouse was on the other side of the valley and it was easy to get lost if you didn't know the way. There was a labyrinth of dirt tracks leading up to the stone wall around the house.

The senator was on time. As he pulled up, he poked his head out the car window and smiled at Glòria. Anna stiffened her neck slightly and momentarily closed her eyes. Glòria got in the back and told them the way.

Back at the house, her husband was awaiting their arrival, having donned a pair of patched dungarees and a straw hat.

'Well, well, well! You sure look like a local!' remarked the senator as they shook hands.

Conrad, with discernible pride, gave them a tour of the garden and the vegetable patch.

'I don't have much time to look after it. But I enjoy seeing it grow. Glòria has more patience. Isn't that right, sweetheart?'

He then proceeded to show them a small plot of sweetcorn and a row of walnut trees lining the stone wall.

'The nuts they produce really are first-class.'

They sat a while on the veranda watching the light change beyond the mountains.

'This is where I do my thinking,' said Conrad. 'At my age, you realise life is divided into wartime and peacetime. You run and run and only now and again do you stop. But it's got nothing to do with age: we do it from the get-go.'

Glòria stood up and went into the kitchen, having said she would prepare a light dinner.

'Hear, hear!' said the senator. 'Best thing in this heat.'

'You absolutely have to taste Glòria's raspberry jam. Aloma said it was to die for…'

They ate in the dining room while gazing at the landscape through the open balcony doors.

'Such silence! Such serenity!' exclaimed the senator. 'Nature returns us to the essence of things. In the city, we live in a permanent state of mania. I guarantee you, if I could, I'd leave it all behind at the drop of a hat! We've lost our taste for the slow passing of time and the changing of the seasons. There's no doubt about it: up here you reconnect with yourself… and with God.'

'Yes, but we're city folk now, people made of concrete and cement,' answered Conrad. 'We can't change. We can't let go of the material world and everything we've accumulated. In fact, I'm thinking of setting up a computer, right here in the farmhouse. The perfect man is a synthesis, after all.'

The two women exchanged a series of nods, first at one husband, then at the other.

'*First I bite the fig then I drink from the fountain…* as one of our most brilliant poets so famously said,' remarked the senator as he waved away the fruit bowl Glòria was offering him.

'Tomorrow we could go to Mass at the Sant Antoni chapel. It's Romanesque and right next to the beech forest,' said Conrad.

'Oh, the beech forest! *La fageda d'en Jordà*! How we've forgotten what our poets have written about our landscape!' said the senator as he lit a Cuban cigar. 'And what about our Romanesque? It's the purest expression of everything our country stands for, from a time when the stones spoke. How the stones of this house must speak. What secrets are they hiding, I wonder…?'

'None anymore,' replied Glòria's husband. 'That was before, when the windows were small and the sound of footsteps echoed between the walls. Before, it was colder, there was more silence, more secrets. Then they buried the past behind a thick layer of lime. We've got more taste in the city but we no longer have any secrets.'

After coffee was served, Glòria went out onto the veranda to sit in one of the wicker armchairs and devote herself to her favourite activity of all: not thinking about anything. She was fond of the night, that kingdom of quiet things. The senator went up to her and stroked her face.

'Counting the stars?' he asked, his hand still resting on her cheek.

'No. I'm just… thinking.'

'This landscape reminds me of you. Imposing from the outside, but once inside, it protects you. You're a formidable woman. You already know how much I admire you. But… *O quam cito transit gloria mundi!*'

Glòria pushed the senator's hand away. Inside there was the sound of footsteps and a prolonged yawn. Anna called the senator. She was tired and wanted to go to sleep. The senator shrugged his shoulders.

'To be continued,' he said and went smiling into the dining room.

Glòria's husband came out and he too stroked her cheek.

'Everything OK?'

'Sure…'

'Shall we hit the hay?'

When they were already in bed and the only sound came from the chirping crickets and the softly creaking beams, Anna yelled: 'Oh, get off, get off me!'

Glòria's husband had been snoring for a while. She placed a hand on his cheek, softly.

Glòria dreamt that she didn't have a house and that she was walking through a bleak, barren landscape. Someone who spoke like Aloma but wasn't Aloma told her she could never return to the house in the valley, that she didn't deserve it, that it was no longer hers. The girl led her to a large, ruined house and told her, from then on, this was her home. Glòria tried to go inside but there was no door, just a narrow hole leading to an entrance hall full of rubble and fallen beams. She slipped through as best she could before going up a staircase with no handrail which led to a dark room without any furniture and with debris piled up on the floor. Glòria lay down on the rubble, closed her eyes and tried to rest.

The chapel interior was a bodiless sea of heads and fans. Glòria was sitting between Conrad and the senator. She heard, as if far in the distance, the congregation answering the priest: 'And with your spirit.' The words and fluttering fans began to lull her to sleep. Then the priest turned and began to read from the Gospel:

'Jesus called his disciples to him and said: "I am come to send fire on the earth and what will I if it be already kindled? But I have a baptism to be baptised with and how am I straitened till it be accomplished! Suppose ye that I am come to give peace on earth? I tell you, nay, but rather division. For from henceforth there shall be five in one house divided, three against two, and two against three. The father shall be divided against the son, and the son against the father; the mother against the daughter, and the daughter against the mother; the mother-in-law against the daughter in law."

'Jesus,' continued the priest, 'who, for the joy that was set before him, endured the Cross, despising the shame, and is set down at the right hand of the throne of God. For consider him that endured such contradiction of sinners against himself, lest ye be wearied and faint in your minds. Ye have not yet resisted unto blood, striving against sin.'

Anna was the only one to take Communion. Glòria noticed how, after receiving the Eucharist, she walked more freely, more supplely. The fans flapped furiously again after the Lord's Prayer. When Aloma was small she loved to imitate how the old ladies fanned themselves, as though her tiny hands were trying to exorcise some vexing demon. That was the first thing she saw when she found her upstairs, in the bedroom overlooking the valley. She saw her stiff hands, no longer fighting against anything. Then she saw the shutters had been closed so the mountains couldn't be seen.

When the priest told them to offer the Sign of Peace, Glòria didn't move. She hadn't heard him. The senator gently turned her towards him and took her hand in his. Glòria noticed it was deathly cold.

All was silent. It had been a while since the senator and his wife had left. Glòria sat in the wicker armchair on the veranda. A strip of fire stretched across the western sky, turning pink with the advancing night. Shepherd's delight, she thought. Inside, Conrad had put *Peer Gynt* on the CD player. Her husband only played classical music at the house in the valley. 'Moments of magic'. What a stupid lie, Glòria thought to herself. There's no magic, no mystery, no secrets anywhere. It was all so predictable, even her pain. Everything had been written.

Conrad came out onto the veranda and switched on the light.

'I don't know why you like sitting in the dark so much…'

he said as he sat down in the wicker armchair next to her. 'The senator's visit has been a stroke of luck. Now he'll definitely oil the wheels regarding my ad campaign.'

'I'm delighted for you…'

'I've invited them up again next weekend, this time with the kids. Don't you find that wife of his, Anna, a tad unsociable?'

'I don't know. We haven't spoken much to one another.'

'You've got a fan in the senator. Anyone with a pair of eyes can see that. Even if he is the perfect mix of a social climber and a sentimental fool. But that's our leaders for you. They talk about landscapes and architecture and poets as if everything belonged to them. Haven't you noticed? *Our* landscape, *our* poets,' said Conrad, mimicking the senator's voice, '*our* Romanesque… But you shouldn't be so standoffish with him. You know full well it helps me to be in his good books.'

'Is that why you went back inside when you saw the two of us on the veranda last night?'

'What do you mean?'

'Nothing. Forget about it.'

'Come on, don't be like that. I didn't see anything.'

Neither of them spoke for a while. By then it was pitch black and there wasn't a single star in the sky.

'Looks like it'll rain tomorrow…'

'Yes…'

'We'll have to head back to Barcelona if it does. The humidity's too much up here.'

'OK,' said Glòria. 'But let me tidy Aloma's room a bit first.'

'We ought to start thinking about turning it into another guest room. It's got the best views, after all.'

'Wait a little. Let's just wait a little longer.'

I DON'T UNDERSTAND SALMON

May this curse end with me!
   SALVADOR ESPRIU, *Antigone*

'It's said that each spring, salmon leave the ocean where they spent the winter. They swim upriver and smash headfirst into the rapids, where some get crushed against the rocks, but others make it before dying in the exact same place they were born.'

'Why, mum? Don't they like the ocean?'

'Yes… but perhaps they find it too big.'

'I like the ocean.'

'Me too.'

'Maybe it's too cold for them as well.'

'Could be.'

'Why do salmon die in the exact same place they were born? How do they remember where to go?'

'Because they have a very good memory. They swim out to sea because it's wide and deep. But later the riverbed calls them.'

'I don't understand salmon.'

Norma felt the cold slicing at her skin. She'd just arrived from the south, where the autumn was still pleasantly warm. She walked along the path leading to the cemetery while the old Republican soldier showed her photographs of his horse, like a grandfather proudly displaying pictures of a grandchild. 'I only get on with animals,' he told her. The cemetery lay nestled within serene surroundings amid meadows and vineyards, outlined by softly sloping hills. A picture postcard image.

Around the edge of the cemetery, someone had planted eighty-one pine saplings. One for each grave. There are people who still recall the February morning when a mass of dirty, bedraggled Republicans appeared.

It's not difficult to remember. The winter was bitterly cold, the rivers froze over, the grapevines were lost and the paths lay thick with sludge. It rained non-stop and mud filled the trenches that the men arriving from the south – half at sea, the lot of them – used as shelter.

The old Republican didn't stop talking. 'My life's like a novel,' he said. 'You know something, Norma? At Mauthausen they made us deportees lug wooden boxes full of shit up from the latrines in the pits where they had us working. Down the steps we'd go, slipping on the ice and muck, they'd saddle us up, and off you went again: the steps, the slope, non-stop. Good luck if you did stop, though!' Norma shivered. The cold felt like someone jabbing a needle into her every pore.

The bodies buried there disappeared for a good number of years. The graves overgrew with bramble and thicket. The names vanished too, hidden deep under the gorse. The French authorities gave every mound a name. Each number was a *rouge espagnol*. The huts at the refugee camp also disappeared, turned into sheds where a farmer kept his tools. The dead had been buried in that plot because they were *rouges*, and the *rouges*, as everyone knows, were barred from the Catholic cemetery.

'Many of the salmon die before they reach their destination. They charge towards the waterfalls and try to jump over them, but often they come crashing down again and the current drags them back out to sea. But they don't give up, because they are very determined. They are so strong they can jump five metres through the air to get over the waterfalls. What's more, they swim against the current.'

'What does "swim against the current" mean?'

They cleared the weeds and, little by little, the mounds began to appear. Each mound they turned into a grave. A grave with a rose and a tombstone. On each tombstone, a name. 'And my horse,' explained the exile, 'whinnies just at the sight of me. He brushes my spine and face with his muzzle and rubs it against my hands. And that makes him happy no end. Then he raises himself up on his hind legs, throws his mane back and fills the valley with his voice.'

Norma looked up at the sky lying low over the mountains, as if wanting to kiss each and every peak. A myriad of green merged with the vineyards. 'And the SS,' continued the Republican, 'dug holes in the ground, twelve feet deep, where they buried the Jews alive. But the only thing I cared about was that box of shit they made me carry. You can't imagine how heavy it got when you were going up those damned steps. I no longer remembered anything, neither the war nor how I'd even ended up in that place.'

Norma felt even colder. She thought about how much she loved him and the desperate desire of their last nights of passion. It was frantic, they went at it again and again, never getting their fill. Norma wanted to run away, to flee that arctic wind. The clouds blotting out the horizon announced an approaching storm. The old man was quiet now. Words were no longer of use; the creeping silence covered everything. The only sound was the wind whispering beyond the vineyards, a soft sound that descended from the mountains. Perhaps it was the murmur of the dead, returning so as not to feel alone.

Someone next to Norma then spoke: 'This here is our flag. Many have died for the Republican flag. But who remembers that now? Who remembers, Norma?' Norma squeezed her eyes shut. From pink to black. She wanted to feel his skin rub against hers, the first contact after a long absence. I'll call him when I get to the hotel, Norma thought. I'll tell him we have to make it better, that I can't forget him, that I don't want to feel pity for the other woman that loves him. Why must it be me who has to forget?

Ghosts accompanied the howl of the unknown dead. The ghosts advanced, retreated, moved in circles. They said nothing. They merely stared with gaping eyes that could never be closed again. We never forget, conveyed their eyes, echoed the murmur. An old man on crutches hobbled towards one of the graves and a fine layer of dust covered the rose resting on the headstone.

Lluïsa, another deportee, had powdered her face as though she were about to perform an 18th Century play. She whispered into Norma's ear: 'We've come from the Têt, the river that carried so many children, women, sick and elderly out to sea. Eight days later the bodies were still washing up on the beach at Argelès. They lay on the sand in silence but the dead are never silent, Norma. Ever.'

Yes, Norma thought to herself, I'll call him from the hotel. I want to hear his voice: I want to hear it, to know he's there, to know he's alive. The old men and women stepped between the gravestones, as if dancing. The pines rocked to and fro, swayed by the slow, silent procession. Then someone spoke on behalf of everyone: 'One of the returning dead, perhaps? We've come here with the same flag we crossed the border with in 1939, something we will never surrender, surrender…'

Norma didn't hear the rest. It was as if the words had been sucked up by the wind. The cold stabbed at her body as though trying to tear through her skin. I'll call you, from so far away, just to say I love you. Surrender, surrender, I love you, I love you. Oh, how I long to feel your soft skin against mine. And your warm kisses, my angel. The sad spirits staggered around her with deep hollows in their cheeks, their swollen skin blackened and dry. It was the dance of death. I wish I could lose all memory and vanish in your waters, receive you as though I were the damp earth along your banks, spread myself over you so you become the sapling and I the tree soaring towards the sky.

The bramble soon colonised the land, turning it into a wilderness. The weeds swallowed up the numbers. The wind blew its death there. The shanties at the camp were destroyed by battering winds and lashing rain. The powdered faces of the phantoms engulfed Norma. She wanted to flee, so not the slightest memory might remain, she wanted to erase… what? Words, perhaps? Norma thought about her angel, more tangible, more real within that dream. She yearned to kiss and be kissed until her dying day.

But, above all, Norma wanted to forget.

'What's more, the females never mistake the river or the place.'

'What? Never?'

'Never.'

'And what about the salmon that don't make it, the ones that get crushed against the rocks?'

'Their bodies are dragged away by the current and thrown back out to sea.'

'Oh, those poor salmon.'

Arsèguel, 1980

THE CHOSEN APPLE

What does falling matter, if we take love with us?
JOSEP CARNER

*Ad te omnis caro veniet**

My hands are full of air yet, in this void, long ago, there could have been a person. A baby, an adult. My child, my lover. But not all mankind.

He is sleeping now. But soon he will call out. Nadiejda. And I will go to him. He says his body itches, that his blood doesn't flow, that it has turned thick like mud.

Before we got married, Madam beckoned me over.

'Young lady, I don't quite know how to tell you this. But there will always be wicked tongues. And wicked tongues never do stop wagging. And these are saying you're not cut out for him. That you've led him down the garden path. I personally don't believe a word of it, but that is what they are saying.'

Of course Madam believed it. She was well-read. She knew Latin. But, above all, she knew what was best for her son.

But we got married, all the same.

We boarded the boat to the island and, during the whole voyage, I told him: 'No.' I told him: 'No' for an entire week. The sea became the sky and the sky became the sea. They had joined in union. Every night he asked me but each time my answer was: 'No.' When I told him: 'No' he would lock himself in the bathroom and begin shaving. Madam had told me the wicked tongues were saying I wasn't cut out for him.

In the bathroom he would recite:

Procul recedant somnia,
Et noctium phantasmata;

*From the Requiem Mass

Hostemque nostrum comprime,
Ne polluantur corpora.

And that is how it was for an entire week. But my soul was irresolute and my body had grown weary. Each night, he would lie by my side and caress me from the tips of my toes up to my hair. 'You know something?' he would then say. 'We begin dying from the soles of our feet.' I told him: 'No' when what I really meant was: 'Yes.'

For years, Madam wrote him letters. I'd take the envelopes, carefully open them with steam and read the contents. But I barely understood what they were about. I knew very little Latin.

Nadiejda! He's calling me again. When we got married, he changed my name. He said I gave him hope – Nadiejda means *hope* in Russian. He barely has a body left. His thin veins seep through his pale skin like braided rivers and his angular nose has become withered and transparent. 'My feet are cold,' he says. I cover him with another blanket. I can hardly see him in the bed under the mountain of blankets.

'You're barely out of swaddling clothes!' Madam told me. 'Nothing but a ditsy little girl. He's a grown man already. He knows what he wants. You, on the other hand, don't even have an education. It's no use hoping you'll reel him in.'

Every night, for an entire week, he locked himself in the bathroom. First on the boat, then at the hotel on the island. And always the same: *Procul recedant somnia...*

When I asked him what those verses meant, he said: 'May we ward off our dreams.'

'Why should we ward off our dreams?' I replied.

He came out of the bathroom and answered me without answering me.

'You're right. Why should we ward off our dreams?'

*May we ward off our dreams, / those nocturnal phantoms; / may the enemy not pollute / our weary body

On the island, I walked up to the sea and begged it to tell me its secret. But the sea would only answer to the wind. And they both laughed at me. 'It's no use hoping,' they said.

In the evening, he would emerge from the bathroom and begin caressing me again. From the tips of my hair all the way down to the tips of my toes. My whole body bore the trace of his kisses.

'You'll see,' Madam went on. 'He's a celebrated critic, a Latinist… a Doctor of Theology, no less! It's no use hoping you'll be happy with him. You won't understand each other. He was still just a small boy and we were already speaking in Latin together. It was our little game. Nobody understood us. Not even his father.'

Now he wants me to bring him a hot-water bottle. There is cold in his bones, he tells me. I check his pulse and feel the slow beats. 'Nadiejda,' he says, 'I'm still holding on.' I kiss his forehead and my lips turn ice cold.

For an entire week, I told him: 'No'. I clamped my legs shut and covered myself with the sheets. Outside, the wind howled with laughter and the sea did nothing to silence it.

He is sleeping now. I bring my ear close and listen to his laboured breathing. His breath seems to come from afar. I've spied a ship about to sink in the black water. I can still take his hand in mine, but it hardly squeezes back anymore. I watch him board the boat, alone. I want to tell him to take me with him but he has locked himself in the bathroom and I can't find the key. I can't open the door; I can't open his eyes and tell him to look at me.

'I never tire of looking at you,' he said on the seventh day. 'I look at you, all of you, but looking is never enough.' On the seventh day, I told him: 'Yes.' He began to kiss me again, all the way from the tips of my toes up to the tips of my hair. Without warning, the wind and the sea fell silent. On the seventh day, I finally said: 'Yes.'

'You're a nice enough girl but you're simply not cut out for him,' said Madam. 'It's no use hoping it'll last. I know my son better than anyone. He enjoys women, naturally, but he soon forgets them. Men like him live their whole lives searching for the ideal woman, the unattainable one. But even if the perfect woman does appear, they discard her as soon as they've got to know her. In the biblical sense, you must understand. Men like him are solitary by nature. The only pleasure they know how to live fully, is intellectual. It's a manner of speaking, but my son would give up half his life for a mere metaphor.'

All he remembers is my name: Nadiejda. Just the other day, he said to me: 'You were blonde when you were younger.' I was brunette. 'And you had the most beautiful neck, like the women in Filipo Lippi paintings.' He had never said that to me before. He always liked my hands and would say: 'They are always full, as if all mankind could fit in them.' But he had never told me my neck was beautiful. It has never been beautiful.

All he remembers is my name. He has forgotten Madam, his friends, all those Latin verses and high-minded thoughts, what day it is, what night. He has forgotten words. Sometimes, he repeats the same one all day long. And then the following day he no longer remembers it. At times it's an entire sentence: 'Roses always seem impossible, and nightingales incomprehensible.' He repeats it as if it were his own. He falls in love with it and then forgets it. Then he begins to say another. And he forgets that too.

He doesn't remember the names of friends, neither the ones still living, of which there are few, nor the ones already passed, of which there are many. Nor the names of his children. Nor the name of the street where he lives, or the city, or the country. One day, I read him the Compline, which he himself had translated into the Catalan, and he told me: 'That's the most beautiful hymn I've ever heard! Read it to me again.' I read it a few more times but a short while later he has already forgotten it.

All he remembers is my name. The one he gave me.

I said: 'Yes' on the seventh day. And on the eighth. And the ninth. I said: 'Yes' for an entire month. The sceptical sea had silently slipped away, while the wind left only the breeze as a reminder. You know something? We begin dying from the soles of our feet. That's why I always kiss you here first.

Nadiejda, I need the toilet. I wrap his gown around him and help him to the bathroom. He walks slowly and hunched over, one agonising step after another. He bumps into a chair. I'm frightened he will break in my hands, that he will shatter into pieces. My hands are full of air. 'I can't go, Nadiejda, take me back to bed.' He is sleeping again. I cover him with the blankets. He looks so small, I lose him in the bed, I can't find his feet.

Three days ago I saw a film on television. It was about a man who lives on an island and whose dog dies. A girl turns up who has lost her shoes and the man, seeing she hasn't any, invites her to stay with him. He treats her like a dog. He humiliates her. The man tosses a bone into the sea and she has to play fetch. He makes her drag herself along the ground, he forces her to walk on all fours, he orders her to lick his outstretched hand. I felt a fire ignite within me and my hands break out into a sweat. I switched off the television.

He was asleep in the bedroom when the sound of my footsteps woke him. 'Nadiejda,' he said, 'I'm departing. My feet are freezing.' I looked over at the photograph on the bedside table. It's of the two of us. Not from when we were on the island, but much later. But we look younger, as though we were meeting again after a long wait. I gaze at his nose, I touch his unblemished skin. There are none of those blue streams. The first time he saw the photograph, he told me: 'We look just like the spouses that meet again after the Last Judgement, all those couples in the fresco at Orvieto Cathedral, do you remember?' I remembered: a man's body and a woman's body embracing one another. Their feet were hidden. As Madam lay on her deathbed, she said to me: 'It's no use holding out for the resurrection of the flesh.'

I picked up the photograph from the bedside table. He was no longer shut away in a dark room. I had the key to unlock the door. I kissed the photograph, crunched it tightly in my fist, and told him: 'Yes' once more. 'Yes. Yes. Yes.'

BEFORE I DESERVE OBLIVION

One's image is always otherworldly.
   MARÍA ZAMBRANO

I'll be watching the water drip,
the vague and gentle ways,
the collected writings and drawn-out drawings
of pain and fortune
– upon dead stones, living faces –
I'll be watching, this and more,
before I deserve oblivion.
   JANOS PILINSZKY, *I'll be watching*

MAY, 1988

One Wednesday evening in the spring of 1978, at between half past six and a quarter to seven to be exact, an incident success-fully kept from the public took place in a secondary school. A teacher of Spanish literature, on the cusp of retirement, was caught hiding in a changing room cupboard by a group of schoolgirls. They had just finished a basketball game and were getting undressed. Without uttering a word to one another the girls un-derstood perfectly well that he'd been spying on them: he was holding a Polaroid camera, after all.

Everyone at school heard about it but the newspapers didn't print as much as one scandalous word on the subject: the teaching body, having called an emergency meeting, decided to keep it from the press. 'It's a delicate case,' announced the Head of Year, 'we're talking about an old man who'll be retiring soon, anyway, what he's done is nothing but ridiculous, all things considered.' 'The onset of dementia,' added the maths teacher. 'A ridiculous thing to do,' repeated the philosophy teacher. 'It's sad,' said the art teacher and specialist in Piero della Francesca. The chemistry teacher, and one of the youngest in the room, screwed her face up: 'Personally, I think it's disgusting.' 'It's not like he raped anyone!' said the ethics teacher, feeling slightly on edge. 'Not this time, no, but what about the next time?' she replied. 'I think we'll have to put him on sick leave for depression,' advised the Head of Year. 'At the end of the day, there's only a few weeks left until the summer holidays and come autumn he won't be here anymore. By then the girls will have forgotten all about it.'

The last comment was uttered by the Head Teacher who, up until that point, hadn't opened his mouth. 'Anyway,' concluded the Head of Year, 'we should thank our lucky stars he's not a senior member of staff and was still on a probationary contract.' 'Senior members of staff don't make fools of themselves in such a humiliating way,' said the maths teacher. They all nodded in agreement, except for the ethics teacher and the art teacher. They weren't senior staff. The chemistry teacher screwed her face up again, but this time she kept quiet: she was only subbing until the end of term.

Roughly an hour later, that is, at around half past seven, a not yet entirely old man shuffled slowly through the Plaça del Rei along the dead stones covering a 6th Century paleochristian cemetery. The passers-by were distracted by the sunset, relishing the warm, mellow light of the long spring evening, without stopping to consider that directly below their feet lay the remains of an ancient burial site.

Neither the not yet entirely old man shuffling slowly nor the strangers strolling leisurely noted the rays of sunshine gilding the gothic stone. We won't either: it has been described too many times for us to walk into the gaping jaws of tautology.

The solitary man was mentally preparing a letter to Joan N, a university acquaintance of mine now working as a secondary school ethics teacher. Joan N was somewhat younger than the man of our story, but ahead of him was a future no less mundane than the old man's past. Joan N did indeed receive a letter, which aspired to be a story, but quickly forgot the whole affair.

The years passed until one day Joan N posted me the letter in question, the one aspiring to be a story sent to him by the old teacher. He'd found it among a pile of old papers when he was moving apartment. It outlined some additional details of the incident, which I mentioned at the beginning. Up to here is all I know.

The letter aspiring to be a story arrived on my desk at the literary journal where I worked. Joan N suggested we publish it: 'Now its protagonist is dead.' The editorial board said it was unfit for publication: not only was it by an unknown author but it was one of those autobiographical texts that nobody wanted to read anymore. The same old dredging up of the past, etc. 'There's nothing interesting about it,' added the Editor-in-Chief, 'neither in terms of form nor content.' 'Form nor content?' I asked. 'No,' he replied, 'it's ponderous, it doesn't skip along.' 'Well, you said it,' I replied, 'if it's ponderous we can't expect it to skip, can we? But what I don't understand is the difference between form and content... aren't they the same thing?' 'Drop it, for Christ's sake,' he replied. I dropped it but I also took the text home with me.

The 'ponderous' text clarified a number of questions from my youth when I had to send my stories and essays – as everyone did who wanted to be published – to the censor. A faceless 'someone', certainly a lot older than I was, would send them back covered in red lines and blue Latin and Greek crosses. They still used a thick, double-sided pencil in those days, similar to the one that always sat on the nun's desk at the school I attended as a girl.

I sent Joan N the standard letter signed by the Editor-in-Chief, the one that reads: 'Dear [enter name],

We regret to inform you that [enter title] does not fit the needs of our journal at this time. Please do not hesitate to contact us should you wish us to return the original.

Yours sincerely, blah, blah, blah.'

He never did request the manuscript. Given that it's you,

the reader, who, at the end of the day, must always have the final word, I leave you a transcription of the text, unedited and unabridged, under the following title:

VARIATIONS ON A POEM BY K

I

Joan, today I had the idea of writing a story but, truth be told, I can't remember the sentence I wanted it to begin with. This happens often to me now. I know that yesterday, as I was strolling through the Gothic quarter, it was a living, breathing sentence, a phrase that tied perfectly with the very last line of the story, a logical phrase that had always been there, suspended in the void, which I plucked out of the air where it hung by a thread, silent but not silenced, so that I might finally make it my own. I could still remember the sentence as I fell asleep in bed. I know how I want the story to end, although the end is something I never want to come to, but I've forgotten the sentence that has to get me there.

If I don't have this sentence, which made me happy and which I gripped as tightly as a tightrope walker does a taut high wire, I won't be able to slip into the nothingness lurking behind the final line. This is the point I want to arrive at. I want to reach the liberating silence. Then, and only then, will the threads be cut, the words tumble, and the air be forever still.

I've never been a storyteller, for the simple reason that I'm incapable of remembering. Admittedly, I do somewhat vaguely recall the alpha of the story: that sentence hanging by a thread in the void. And I can still clearly visualise the omega, it's just everything in between that I've forgotten. I remember being a child who was no more than a child and I remember yesterday but everything in between is repetition. And what comes in between, that's to say adulthood, is that to which God condemns those of us who lack imagination.

I'm lying, because between the brackets of oblivion are K's poems, as well as my thick red lines and blue Latin and Greek crosses made with my double-sided pencil: my lines and my crosses through the words and the phrases of others. I was charged with exterminating them.

But I wasn't the executioner, merely his assistant. The words of others arrived on my desk woven into a story like so many others and perhaps even as old as the origins of the world. Those who murdered people came before me. My job was to massacre words, a crime that goes unpunished given it's not recognised by any legal system or criminal code. Not that I ever considered myself a criminal, nor was there anything mysterious about my mission. If anything it was prosaic and repetitive. Words don't cry out or suffer like people. They are incapable of lamenting. No one has ever described their agony, nor have words ever written about their own pain. My job was to obliterate stories conceived by other minds, words written by individuals who obstinately insisted on continuing to weave them into stories. In my eyes, these faceless strangers were guilty of deluding their readers, of making them believe they could access another, imaginary, universe. They were guilty of striving to make real the invisible universe of the written word.

The world was small back then. It had limits and borders. We, the survivors, only needed ourselves. But then storytellers came along and made it big by bombarding its limits with imagination and carrying readers headlong into the eye of the storm. I had to help reduce the world once again, to return it to its previous calmness. I read the beautiful, everlasting stories written by strangers but, in order to survive, I had to forget them. If I'd maintained any memory, I'd have been done for. That is why I only have the beginning, which I don't remember, and the end, which I do.

In the beginning, I was a child who was no more than a child. Now I'm a man not yet tired enough to die. But I don't feel old.

It's the world, Joan, that has grown old around me. Our perception grows old, our environment decays, the air turns heavy and dense, but us? No, we never get old. Anyway, who cares if the body deteriorates as long as one's spirit stays strong? The last thing to get old, Joan, is the heart. I remember you agreeing with me the first time I told you this.

The poems composed by K (I'm not referring, by the way, to the book about Josef K! That I leave to those who take pleasure in analysing others people's terror) arrived on my desk in the form of a beautifully bound typescript, devoid of any additional footnotes, but containing a short synopsis by the translator. One hundred and fifty-four poems written by K between 1911 and 1933, supplemented by twenty-four verses from before 1911, and thirteen from K's personal archive.

The tone of the translator's introduction was too highbrow to be understood by readers in those days, reasoning that if I didn't understand it then neither would they, and after skimming it I picked up my thick double-sided pencil – red at one end, blue at the other – and turned the page, ready to get to work on the first poem. It was pre-1911 and called *Longings*. As I read it, my grip on the pencil gradually loosened. I read it twice more before closing the beautifully bound text and placing it at the far end of my desk.

Next, I tried my hand at a crime novel set in Barcelona's red light district. I drew a red line through the word 'pit' and replaced it with 'underarm', I took out the word 'breasts' each time it appeared, and with the blue end of my pencil I crossed out three pages that meticulously described the act of fornication, writing in the margin a colossal 'NO'.

But I couldn't concentrate. Those words kept invading my thoughts and rather than having read them it was if they were suspended in mid-air, provoking me, luring something up from a bottomless pool: *so appear the longings that have passed, so appear the longings that have passed, so appear the longings that have passed.* I was tense and nervous and decided to focus my efforts on the crime novel, all too easy to chop into pieces. I was an old hand. Mutilating the pages of a crime novel was to me what pairing quantum numbers is to an atomic physicist. But it was impossible. The words began to swoop down on me again: *without being satisfied, not one of them granted, without being satisfied, not one of them granted.* I finished work for the day and looked over at the far end of the desk. There was the typescript containing K's poems. I took it home with me and read the one hundred and sixty-seven poems in a single night. Poems penned by an Alexandrian poet who, in his youth, had been athletic and not unhandsome. And I, the man with no memory, learnt *Longings* by heart.

K's words didn't deserve to be betrayed. But that is what I did every morning at my dismal desk in the darkest corner of a dilapidated room – our proximity to the window reflecting the established hierarchy between us – where other men without a memory had sat before me.

Men who went on living because they didn't remember, because they had forgotten language and discarded the material needed to form words. Other men, similar in every way to me, sat behind the same dismal desk in the same dilapidated room, drawing red lines and blue crosses, both Latin and Greek, through words formed by those who hadn't forgotten this raw material and fought tooth and nail to keep it alive. And there is surely nothing more dangerous than a writer who never knows when they are beaten. Mine were lines drawn with violence but never with hatred. At the end of the day, hate ennobles. We had to be like the strong northern gales, unrelentingly eroding their defences, not with the wind's secular slowness but with hurricane force. I write like this now, but back then we didn't think in such poetic terms: those red lines and blue crosses put food on the table. We hunted words one by one, stripping them of their context, never stopping to consider the unique atmosphere of each novel, despite suspecting they were getting their revenge on history. Or that, quite possibly, they were history itself.

We had nothing but our own fear, and the best way of countering it was with oblivion. I had to forget the fact that all those beautiful, everlasting stories stacked on my desk had been written with the hope of the eternally hopeful, with the hope of those who required it to go on living. Now I'm an old man I can assert with candidness (because old men retain the right to be candid) that the others, that herd of faceless names, believed wholeheartedly in every word they wrote. They were more determined than us, sat at our dreary desks, some closer to the window, others further away.

Their typescripts stacked on my desk spoke to me of sleepless nights, the nonexistence of weekends or holidays, the internal struggle to unearth and nurture their talent, if indeed they had any, the incomprehension of everything around them, and their own terrible, pulsating anguish. But they believed in what they were doing; they had faith. I didn't believe in the violent red lines I scarred their pages with each morning. Who knows? Perhaps I really did hate them. I suspected they were mocking me, ridiculing my red lines and blue crosses, laughing at my law, at my very existence. They could live without me, but I couldn't live without them. I was tied to them. It would only come to an end on the day that their – occasionally – beautifully bound typescripts were no longer stacked on my dreary desk in the darkest corner of the room, as far as one could get from the light.

II

Back when I was a child who was no more than a child and words came fearlessly to me, stripped, at times, of the meaning afforded them by adults, I was given a kaleidoscope. For a few days, I hardly uttered a word and all of my efforts I channelled into not speaking. My mind and my eye homed in and concentrated on the colours and shapes coming together and falling apart forming, on occasion, harmonic, on others, fractured combinations. With only the slightest movement of my finger, this harmony would come crashing down, and it was my eye that either fixed it or destroyed it once and for all. I had the capacity to create order only to convert it into chaos. And it was my mind, guiding my eye, that did it. But the shapes created by the kaleidoscope were not me, so I soon got bored with it. I'd then go down to the river and sit on the bank where a pool formed in one of its bends. I entertained myself by dropping pebbles into the water and watching my own seemingly endless image. I was all the children in the world, an infinite ego, composed of all those faces reflected in the pool, faces that flowed continuously into another until the water became still and I started again. When I drew red lines and blue crosses through the words of others, it was as if I were seeing all those faces again, rippling across the page.

When I got tired of seeing the sequence of faces floating in the water I'd return to my kaleidoscope. But neither the images reflected in the river, nor the colourful combinations of the kaleidoscope carried me any closer to words.

It's impossible for any of us to recall when we first learnt to look. Our retina doesn't leave an imprint of those original images in our memory. Likewise, we don't remember the first time we see our reflection in the mirror, the 'other' with whom we come to associate ourselves. If some part of our supressed memory were returned to us, no doubt we would have a different idea of ourselves. Discovering we are objects, we would search for the exact word and stop treating others as mere objects, fully aware of what we represent to them. Yet my memory of searching within the shimmering waters of the pool for my imprisoned ego is crystal clear, for it was an ego that attempted to free itself by multiplying almost infinitely.

I want to leave these tiring thoughts behind: they are useless at my age. At some point, I'll have to make a U-turn and return to what took place yesterday, far closer to me in time. And there will be no stop-offs to admire each season of my life, not if I can't remember them. It's funny how, long after the event, we insist on calling them 'seasons' despite the fact that they never follow our memory's linear logic when we are actually living them. Whereas people used to stubbornly insist upon dividing their lives into 'chapters', born out of the habit of reading novels, nowadays they transplant this ready-made structure onto their personal vision of the world due to television series. Before they deluded themselves with literature, now they dupe themselves with images that deliver them from the here and now and whisk them away to far-flung places. That is what I'd think about as I went about putting thick lines through the beautiful, everlasting stories written by strangers with a name but no face. I, the destroyer of words, knew how to look. But I couldn't tell anyone.

Yesterday, a group of secondary school girls caught me hiding in the changing room cupboard looking at them through a gap in the door. I was holding a Polaroid camera. I've learnt to take pictures of the present. By photographing them, I possessed them. I can imagine the Catalan language teacher's horrified reaction and I can hear the chemistry teacher saying I'm nothing but a filthy voyeur who rapes with his eyes. But is either woman capable of conceptualising photography as representing the modern ritualisation of a virgin's deflowering? Not that it matters what they think. I have not invented anything. All possible stories have already been written.

For a number of years, I entertained myself by cutting out passages on this very subject that I myself had censored. I keep them at home in a drawer. And now I have the urge to transcribe one such passage for you:

The contact of a pure body, never before touched by a lover's hands, has a unique, peculiar coolness within its tension, a clumsiness that nevertheless hits the mark, a candidness that intuits, adapts and finds, by dark means, attitudes that meticulously and *intimately interlock members. Sheltered within my sweetheart's embrace, her timid skin seeming to harden upon my thigh, my rage over having exhausted my flesh with so many worn-out relationships was roused, along with the absurd pretension of finding future repose in present excesses (...) The idea of a virgin giving herself to me, and the intact, closed flesh demanding a slow and sustained effort on my behalf, filled me with the fear of failure.* *

The author of these words, describing what it means to touch a virgin for the first time, is considered one of the foremost writers of the 20th Century. As such, they readily forgive him the exact same indiscretion they are unwilling to forgive me: the audacity of having converted a common thought among men into something material. For what man has never dreamt of deflowering a virgin? Why is my gaze guiltier than his words? Was the writer not, in that precise moment, conveying his own most private longings?

Naturally, my act lacked the grandeur necessary for great art. The nymphets were not at all frightened and merely fell about laughing when they caught me hiding in the cupboard and contemplating them through a gap in the door.

Now I remember the sentence I was supposed to begin the story with:

Before you is an old man, not yet tired enough to die, who watches little girls as they get undressed, who are unaware they are being watched by a satyr, also not yet tired enough to die...

Subordinate clauses always sound good at night. But in narrative terms, the kaleidoscope and its harmonised images shattering just as they take shape is far more alluring. In the daytime, subordinate clauses shatter all by themselves. In the daytime, the world demands simple sentences, subject-verb-object, full stop,

*Alejo Carpentier, *The Way of Saint James*

new paragraph, while adjectives are to be austere, precise and to efficiently complement the verb. As the terse prose of day takes over, nocturnal rhetoric begins to feel inhibited and awkward. At night, anyone who dreams can be a poet but during the day only a few are writers who write. Prose, then, admits no excuses: this is not about an old man not yet tired enough to die but a bad literature teacher spying on schoolgirls as they get undressed. The precise adjective is 'ridiculous'.

The child who observed his multiplicitous ego in the waters of the pool is now an old man who yesterday made a group of schoolgirls laugh. At that precise moment, I wasn't an infinitely expanding ego but a risible object.

The purpose of this story isn't to provoke compassion. For the first time in my life, I'm filling my inner emptiness with words. And the person doing it is a man who has never written anything before because all he knew how to do was look.

I know, I know. I'm making a mess of it. And you, Joan, to whom this story is humbly addressed, are no doubt expecting a coherent explanation for yesterday's events. If my explanation were indeed coherent, psychologists could add it to their studies on what growing old means for a man in this day and age. Only old people understand that decadence is an atemporal phenomenon. It's all the same to me if they choose to hide the bare bones of our decrepitude, the decline of our aptitudes, our neglected appearance and loss of memory behind imbecilic euphemisms because, at the end of the day, only old people can speak for themselves. Every old person is different, unique. Solitary. Let the sociologists and psychologists tell us what it means with their statistics and theories that become obsolete every ten years. What they fail to see is that every old person has their own voice. The verisimilitude of the self can only to be expressed through stories. After all, what is a story if not a parody of life?

But I'm too late. All I can do now is grip tightly as I, a tired destroyer of words, go from order to chaos, just like the kaleidoscope of my childhood. Uninterrupted order in a story is disingenuous. I learnt that much from reading the manuscripts that made their way into my dark corner: many of them were too ordered to be believable. I learnt it then but I only know it now, just as life is slipping from my grasp and I desperately hold onto it with the help of a few words.

III

Joan, you're the only one who ever showed me any kindness at school, despite it only coming in the form of a robotic greeting. But you have no idea how much I appreciated your conventional, absent-minded: 'Good morning'. I know I haven't been a good teacher. But I don't believe it has anything to do with my past as a mutilator of images and words. It's also worth noting that neither you nor the others ever censured me for my previous employment, at least not to my face. Not that you had much information to go on, of course. You knew that I knew that you all knew but, like everyone, you wanted to forget. Some of those who did the same as me are now prize-winning novelists or acclaimed men of letters while others, in the winter of life, go about with the insatiable geniality of those who have attained universal oblivion. There is nothing more magical than geniality; it's the morbid influence of our times. Geniality is the result of forgetting. It's a half-open mouth only suggesting, but never showing, its fangs. A genial smile is like a cannibalistic rictus. After all, it was genial people who taught me how to draw red lines and blue crosses, the symbols that signed the death sentences for the words of the faithful. As I've already told you, years ago they used to murder people but it wasn't necessary for murderers to be genial. The phenomenon of geniality is better suited to times of peace.

In many ways, I wasn't so dissimilar from the strangers who sent me their typescripts, the only real distinction was that those masters of metaphors and images had inserted their dreams and desires – some more successfully and with decidedly more talent than others – into the texts that I'd later hold in my ungainly hands. Their dreams, their desires and their nostalgias: 'The melancholic and nostalgic outpouring of thwarted love and lost youth,' as you would often say. You always spoke so well, Joan. Given your fine memory, you were able to recite Eugeni d'Ors, word for word.

Who knows if these writers, some of whom were held in high esteem and even translated into foreign languages, soared high upon their own desires once the world realised that my mission, and that of others like me, was powerless to smother talent when it's constant and unbending? Longings destined to pass without being satisfied, as K wrote. Is this where literature proposes the possibility of reconciliation? Is it here where one begins to develop a sense of compassion? They were architects, master craftsmen and labourers all at once; they practiced every trade involved in building their beautiful, everlasting stories. And then I'd come along with an excavator and raze them to the ground. But don't make the mistake of attributing my – *our* – actions to any noble sentiments or studied theories. We did it to eat. The majority of us were starving to death. I was employed to do a specific job, which I did well, but I wasn't fulfilling any personal calling. There was nothing sublime about it. When concentrating on the words of others and what they did and didn't say, I was, in reality, enlarging the images behind each word as if, with an electron microscope, searching for the most microscopic insinuation of what K sang about in the farthest, most clandestine corners of my consciousness. And contrary to what you may think, it wasn't the chapter with veiled insults against the motherland that I homed in on, or the discreet irony aimed at 'military honour', or the sarcasm shrouded in anachronisms targeting our generals' imagined heroism, but that which gave off the scent of sex.

What, exactly, gives off the scent of sex? That is something contemplators like me cannot answer.

Ancient philosophers assert that the soul is in the stomach. And I must say I agree with them. When it comes to our bodies' response to the chemistry of love, the principal organ isn't the heart. Pathetic, pusillanimous, pre-packaged romanticism! It's the stomach. Why? Because the stomach has no pulse, no memory.

Ah, the chemistry of love! Do you remember when you talked to me about it? You said: 'A kiss is nothing but chemical substances flooding our brain's pleasure centres,' adding, 'we still don't have the full equation, but we do have a number of its algorithms.' For instance, the organism of a human in love produces large quantities of a chemical compound similar to adrenaline. The receptors in specific areas of the body trap, dissolve and assimilate it, altering certain functions and stimulating a dynamic response in the central nervous system, turning the person into what is more commonly known as "a bag of nerves". And it's these neurochemicals that cause compatibilities and incompatibilities between individuals which, according to you, is why we should employ the language of junkies: people in love go around 'high', they display all the symptoms and it's dangerous for them to not get their 'fix'. The procurers and brothel-keepers of yesteryear are the drug dealers of today, of which plenty are involved in the business of love, all of which led you to your conclusion: when a relationship ends, the scarcity of the neurochemicals that had sustained the sensation of love can cause PTSD. (It's worth mentioning here that the only person who showed any real interest in your theory was the science teacher. To me it was little more than the stereotypical thinking – that is, loose and lacking life experience – of the young philosopher unfortunate enough to live in the doldrums of modern thought and who has ended up teaching ethics to a bunch of teenagers incapable of producing any other discourse than the one they see on TV.)

And just like that, you reduced the greatest of human passions to a simple question of pharmaceutics. But you are much younger than I am, Joan, and you live in an era where pleasure has been theorised to such a degree that afterwards you don't know how to experience it properly. When you told me this, I immediately thought of K's verses. How I'd have liked to have been able to recite them to you:

> *Like the beautiful bodies of those who died before growing old,*
> *sadly shut away in a sumptuous mausoleum...*

Thus I put red lines and blue crosses through the words of strangers while my stomach, lacking a pulse, contracted. And instantly the diurnal adjective reappears, intolerant of the musical prosody of subordinate clauses. *Ridiculous*. Ridiculous: the person who goes around high on love; ridiculous: the person who never has.

The unknown narrators liberated my multiplicitous ego, each identity bearing a story built with thousands of words simultaneously shattering into tens of thousands of possibilities. They were the voices of those who didn't fear me, who mocked and ignored me, the faint voices that came from afar to laugh at my thick double-sided pencil. The voices of those who soared joyously above the void like nocturnal thieves, stealing souls from humanity to return them to literature. *Joie de vivre*, sir, as a poet with a sentimental streak would no doubt say.

Meanwhile, my stomach got smaller and smaller, suffocating my soul until it finally succumbed.

When I was a child who was no more than a child, I looked and objects came to me. Houses, silhouetted in the dark night with chimneys like the tall towers of a castle, came to me. The still visible moon, inhabited by vampires, came to me. All things came to me, including her, though I no longer recall if she was walking or on horseback. Let's just say she came on horseback. Let's say she came like Lady Godiva, riding bareback, the horse raising itself up on its hind legs and filling the valley with its voice. Perfect. And that is in spite of TV adverts having ruined this image for us: on far too many occasions have we seen wild horses galloping freely through lush meadows or alongside crashing waves. Poetic images are dead, move on, nothing to see here. But I preserve the right to lie, just like the authors of all those beautiful, everlasting stories. If we were forced to re-enact everything they wrote, transported by their enthusiasm for confabulation, we'd see that that bunch of supressed souls wasn't nearly as supressed as they like to make out nowadays, and that they were capable of referencing a whole range of pleasures. That was when my red and blue pencil didn't draw... it flew.

I followed her. The girl on horseback advanced along a dirt path and it wasn't long until she gave herself to me. As I was possessing her, the faces from the pool went rippling over her body.

I possessed her but I didn't look at her. The beholder only looks when he has nothing left to lose. All the girls sat before me in class over the years were her. 'I' had multiplied into a thousand selves, one for each of the stories I'd had to read, but they had been condensed into a single 'you'. That is how it's always been between man and woman. The girls were her, that body I possessed one summer's day when the sky turned the colour of naked barley – when recounting love scenes that took place outside, you always have to give the sky a different colour.

So, as I was saying, I followed her along the dirt path, up to the tiny chapel. We pushed through the undergrowth and as I went running beside her I contemplated her legs. When we reached the chapel we were both short of breath. Below us spread a sea of mountains made of a million emerald hues and, beyond them, a monumental blue stain. It was the Pyrenees. The entrance to the chapel was half in ruins, grass had invaded the apse and weeds had long colonised the roof. Inside there were just a few pews and a small altar covered with a threadbare cloth. A plaster- cast saint stared back at us with an incredibly dim-witted look on its face giving it a distinct resemblance to father's middle-aged, bachelor brother. Outside, by the stone wall, there was a row of niches piled one on top of the other. Some of the names were missing letters, as though their bearers weren't completely dead. White cows grazed in the meadows and, high up on the hilltop, a large house in ruins clung to existence. The oaks twisted as if tormented by some inner evil while the sun descended behind a still snowy mountain peak leaving behind a body of frothy, weightless clouds. The sound of a cattle bell and barking reached us as we climbed higher towards the edge of the abyss, an abrupt abyss, full of gorse. A lizard tickled her feet, making her laugh, and I leant forward and kissed her. There is nothing quite like a kiss standing before a sea of mountains. So, tell me, was our kiss nothing but chemical substances flooding our brains' pleasure centres?

IV

I remember hearing you and some colleagues commenting once on the girls' transformation. When they arrive in October, they are babes still, with imperceptible hairs on their bare arms, and pink, pale lips. They sit innocently but provocatively, their little legs wide apart, their skirts halfway up their thighs, and their chins resting on one hand, with nothing to conceal. So small, yet so insolent. This is when they study the great minstrel archpriest, Gonzalo de Berceo, who sang devotional works in praise of the Holy Virgin to the delight of saints and sinners alike.

Halfway through the autumn, the change commences, albeit almost undetectable. Their chests are no longer quite as flat, they slump forward slightly as if not understanding the new weight and… What was my point? Ah, yes, the maestro of medieval monophony:

> *Where'pon I sang many a cantiga*
> *For Moors, Jews and the odd believer.*

When winter arrives, their legs are hidden under trousers and thick tights. This is when they read the mystics. By the time we get to *Life is a Dream*, they are already women... whether they are conscious of it or not.

> *Does possessing a superior soul*
> *Make me less free?**

Their young bodies, constricted by tight blouses, burst forth, their thighs trace a delirious curve and their faces, even more insolent than before, exude a brightness the extent of which they are completely unaware. We've got a little more like old men and they a little more like young women.

I've not been able to focus on what I teach for a long time. I repeat the same texts apathetically year after year, remembering them only in class. Immediately afterwards I erase all memory of them. We forget the things that don't move us. All I remember are K's verses: *like the beautiful bodies of those who died before growing old*... Perhaps it's because I carry their meaning hidden deep in the furthest reaches of my stomach.

Men such as me are like antique furniture that has never been in fashion. However, should the unlikely day come when these obscure pieces are in vogue, no one would know what they had been originally used for. Men like me live only a single story and, when it's finished, everything else is repetition. The day she departed, with the same joy with which she had arrived, I was left feeling sullen. Not sad; sullen. They rob you of your self and never return it, and the stories that come afterwards are nothing but agonising, fruitless searches for the first. The original. Nevertheless, our body, betraying and misleading the multiplicitous ego, offers no answer.

Could that be the reason I drew red lines and blue crosses, both Latin and Greek, through other people's stories with such wrath? The story of the boy who meets a girl on a dirt track and

*Life is a Dream, by Calderón de la Barca

takes her to an abandoned chapel has many variations, from the urban alley underneath the glare of a neon sign, to a room with an interior design as false as the situation. Needless to say, in our dreams she never fails to offer herself up to us, completely naked. The sky takes on many colours because, as I've already mentioned, the sky is a timeworn literary device: the crisp, rural sky cut through by mountain peaks; the cloudy, frothy sky of the high seas; the hazy, city sky and its golden obscurity. When two bodies embrace, there is always a moment when we look up to the sky, even if our gaze only collides with the bedroom ceiling, reminding us it needs a fresh coat of paint. Nowhere is there a pool in which you might contemplate yourself; nowhere is there a pool offering you an escape.

The storytellers sent me her arrival in a variety of scenes, as though they had relived a story belonging to me. But the original fabulist had already stolen it from me long before the temptation story was invented. Whether I knew it or not, I'd long been banished from the kingdom of words, meanwhile all the eager scribes sent my own story back to me dressed in modern language. She was in every word, every image, leaping from the page to mock me, rising up to remind me of what had once been but could be no more.

But please, let us return to the matter at hand, the one you must all be commenting on in the staff room. 'Surely he could be kept on!' exclaims the maths teacher. Someone implies it's all down to testosterone, that 'wicked hormone' capable of leading even the purest of hermits into temptation. Someone else – the PE teacher, perhaps? – doesn't agree. According to him, I'm a textbook case of necrospermia. The chemistry teacher screws her nose up, bestowing upon her a certain piquant quality. She is much prettier than she realises, you know. She tells you all to stop complicating things so much and that, like the majority of men, I only have one thing on my mind. As usual, the Headmaster holds his tongue, and the one calling the shots is the Head of Year. I imagine at some point the philosophy teacher, fresh from his stay in Tübingen, won't be able to resist saying something along the lines of: 'But at what junction does one's true self come into view? Must the subjective mind lie forever concealed?' Given you've never studied abroad, you make a monumental effort not to laugh out loud. The philosophy teacher's obsession with parapsychology and, being the good Aristotelian that he is, his secret admiration for Count Cagliostro, are common knowledge. But none of you says what all of you are thinking: that, at the end of the day, I'm nothing but a washed-up old man.

Someone else – perhaps the Catalan language teacher, this time – will remember favourably that I'm married and, naturally, express her surprise at my behaviour: a married man doesn't normally commit such 'ridiculous' acts. She can't bring herself to utter the word 'obscene'. She might be aware of the grammar of the Catalan language, but its art is lost on her.

But she would be right to be surprised. After all, I do have a good wife at home. A real first-class shadow. While other women give, take and disappear, wives like mine are sad caricatures of the one that got away. My wife is the other's shadow, but the other is me. I can't help picturing her stiff upper lip, her languid reaction and subsequent resignation when she realises what her husband has been caught doing and its inevitable consequences. To cut a long story short: disciplinary action or early retirement.

Some of us are condemned at birth to a life of looking. That is why I was so good at my job: for he who looks, censors. Or do you contend that there is any other way of looking? I myself saw it once, so perhaps I'll discuss it further on. When I was a small boy, I'd peek through the gaps in the floorboards above my parents' bedroom. On more than one occasion I watched them fuck (please, don't oblige me to use the French affectation and say 'make love', not when we've come this far!). My retina quickly grew accustomed to the darkness and my pupils dilated, just like my veins under the pressure of my accelerating rage. People pay such little attention to dilating pupils. Devoid of all thought, I watched my parents lie together before my father turned and mounted my mother. My stomach, up until that moment unfeeling, began to fill with nervous energy and to convulse like the groaning horseman below. I possessed my mother, until noticing my hand was wet, just as my father collapsed upon her lifeless body, embracing him like the earth is destined to embrace us all.

I recalled this scene the day of my father's funeral. As they lowered his coffin into the open earth, I pictured my mother underneath him, the two of them locked in a kiss of death.

I said before that she arrived on horseback, but I've still not given you any details. She did appear on horseback, that much is true, but the horse wasn't white and she wasn't naked. All the lads were looking as she paraded herself in front of us. Next to her was a mournful-looking bear playing the cymbals and behind her a sickly, skeletal chimp comically attempting a few forward rolls. She'd arrived with the travelling circus, wearing a red coat decorated with golden epaulettes and shiny brass buttons, her long hair cascading down her back, and a body as slender as bulrush.

That night we watched her perform solo on the trapeze (she was the only trapeze artist in the ramshackle circus) in a pair of flesh-coloured tights. Hanging from the bar, she seemed made of air, her fiery red mane floating like an autumn leaf on the wind. All of us were looking at her and having her. I took my father's binoculars in order to get a close up of her and they went passing from one pair of eager hands to another. The autumn leaf metamorphosed into a butterfly, assimilating all of nature's colours so as not to be devoured by some lurking predator: the branches of a dead pine, the bark of a trunk, the leaves of a Japanese plum tree… The combination of colours depended on how the sun would caress her as it crept through the patched tarpaulin. I remember deciding that she flew so high because she was scared: up there no one would be able to harm her.

The following night I went back to see her. I didn't let anyone else touch the binoculars and I spent the entire show with my gaze fixed solely on her. Afterwards in bed, the image of the girl, as she glided through the air, still permeated my retina. I couldn't sleep. During bouts of insomnia, especially when our body is not yet fully mature, there are fleeting moments when a universal consciousness comes to us. It's an ephemeral vision we are forced to turn away from, and if it came to us on a regular basis we would surely die of fright. The only people capable of bearing it are those who believe themselves to be the chosen ones, men hand-picked to perform great deeds. That is why I pictured the girl swinging high up on the trapeze. My hands became tangled in her mass of hair the colour of Japanese plum blossom. I kissed her rippling red mane until I was overcome with exhaustion, leaving every inch of her body covered in my kisses. Mine and mine alone. And then I had her. I had her like I've never had any other woman since.

But still I couldn't get to sleep. Through the window came a spectacular glow, as though a lost soul had collided with the glass. I opened the window and heard the whistling wind deride me. The wind has always seemed like an adversary. The yellow lights of the travelling circus danced in the distance and far, far above, Sirius shone uncompassionately. The huge star devoured both the circus lights and the woman I longed to possess. No one believes in the stars' cosmic magnetism anymore, partly because we can no longer see them. As a youngster, I'd sneer at the inept city poets and how they used the stars as a resource without realising that such devices were doomed to fail. But back then I was still convinced that when a man falls in love for the first time the whole sky reverberates with his longing. A falling star proved it to me.

I leapt out of the window and strode towards the blinking lights, attracted by their dance and driven by my own desire. Deep in the night the dogs barked and the crickets chirped as if warning of an intruder. The travelling circus was composed of only four wagons. In one of them they kept the decrepit monkeys, and the mournful bear with fur like a filthy, moth-eaten rug. The second and third wagons were both shrouded in darkness, but the fourth, slightly apart from the rest, emitted a flickering yellow light as though from the flame of a dying candle. I edged towards it and looked through the window. On the right, pinned to the wall, was an image of Saint Pancras. On the left, towards the far end of the wagon, was a bed. Lying on it was my father cloaked in a pair of copper coloured wings. She had him pinned to the mattress but the rhythmic movement of her body made it seem as though she were simultaneously trying to take off, break through the roof and carry my father away into the night sky. They were both laughing.

An intuitive voice told me they were laughing because they both knew that one day they would die.

I envisioned my own death and had the premonition that it had already begun. If I hadn't seen them laughing – because I didn't hear them, I only saw them – I wouldn't have envisioned my own death. Nevertheless, it began there and then. But I felt it with none of their joy. *They were laughing because they both knew that one day they would die.*

I envied their defiance, their recklessness. It was the same sentiment I'd go on to recognise in the texts it was my job to silence. I didn't cross out words with a sense of religious righteousness. No, that would have been far too easy: I assailed them with my pencil because I was envious. And what I envied was the creative act in its purest state.

I stood rooted to the spot, relishing what I saw through the gap between the window and the wooden shutter, participating in the destructive yet creative force of my father and the gypsy girl. I watched them fixedly without blinking. Every movement, every act, every jolt, remained etched forever in my mind's eye with the exactness of an entomologist who studies the short lifespan of some tiny insect. I became both my father and her, rolling with them, desiring with them, immersing myself in the ripples of the pool. I became all of my identities. I transformed into everything that reproduces itself upon this Earth and beyond, where the stars fall.

When it was over and they slowly sank into a mutual, earthy embrace, I ran away to lie down near the dirt track, my head resting on a stone amid the decaying flora.

I lay there for a long, long time, ordering the series of images, one by one, until they were safely stored in my brain. I'd also played a part in that story and I wanted to always remember it. My role had been that of the beholder. A cloud of stars fell down upon me, whispering wild promises of infinity while devouring me.

All at once, I stood up knowing exactly what I was going to do. I didn't think or say to myself: this is what you should to do, and then this, etc. No, that's not how we speak to ourselves. I simply listened to the voice in my stomach. Did you know that the ancients believed the voice of love and the voice of vengeance to be bedfellows?

Mother was already in bed, sound asleep, a thin trail of saliva slipping from one corner of her mouth. It was a sweet, unsuspecting sleep, the sort we often mistake for innocence. I brushed my thumb lightly over her skin and she stirred slightly, as if expecting it. Then I shook her awake and, opening one eye, she asked me what I wanted. I told her everything. I didn't spare her a single detail. I only hid my brief encounter with the stars, for if I'd told her that she wouldn't have believed the rest. She no doubt trotted out the same line as always: 'You little liar, you! Too much imagination for your own good!' What neither of us knew was that all writers were liars as children, the ones that sent me their texts being no exception. She closed her eye and waved me away, telling me to go back to my room. It had been but a dream. Too much imagination for my own good. But not only did I know she'd believed every word, I also knew that, from that moment onwards, my father's dreams would turn to stone.

The following day the police came to arrest everyone in the travelling circus. They didn't have a permit and someone had reported them. The sad, ramshackle circus was illegal. The gypsy girl was crying, or at least I thought she was. Her hair was in a bun and was no longer the colour of copper. As she was bundled away, amid the decrepit chimps and the morose bear, I caught sight of my father's eyes. They weren't eyes that looked but eyes that loved (I shall return to this image later on).

Not long after that, father disappeared. Rumour was he'd headed east, towards the coast, in search of the flying circus girl. Word was he never found her. I stayed with mother until she sent me to study in the city, where I lived with my uncle and his wife. By that point I already knew I'd never seek another the way I sought the girl from the travelling circus.

v

Above I write that I guided her along the dirt track, towards the tiny chapel, whereupon I had her. But I invented this story; I invented it with my father's gaze from when I saw his eyes following the girl from the travelling circus. I had her with my father's eyes but not with his hands. That I merely refashioned from the beautifully bound typescripts sent to me by all the devoted descendants of the original fabulist.

Mother took father in again when he returned to the village, looking much older than he really was and desperately ill. My mother's revenge, or perhaps her triumph, was to aid him in dying a good death, while overseeing the transformation of a once infatuated man into a penitent one. It wasn't difficult and there is always a time in life when we participate in reducing someone to nothing. I never saw my father again. Not even after he died. I arrived the very day of the funeral, just in time to see them lower the coffin into the damp earth, near the niches with the names spelt incorrectly, by the chapel at the top of the dirt track of my dreams, along which I'd guided the girl from the travelling circus. I arrived at that ceremony of absolution just in time to contemplate the coffin as it disappeared.

For as long as those typescripts kept arriving on my dismal desk in my dark corner I went on searching in them for my story. I assumed that they – and by 'they' I mean the army of inventors of images and metaphors, the flag bearers of hope – also lived like me, forced to contemplate. The gateway of light is the eye, for the eye that looks is the eye that illuminates reality. They also spied through a gap, eyeing longings that passed without being satisfied, as K says.

I've already said that I felt no hatred, but that isn't true. I hated them because in each text I caught a glimpse of the snitch cowering in me, the informer incapable of keeping a secret to himself in order to recount it later on. That is precisely what secrets are for: to be transformed later into fragments of a re-imagined past. The fabulists also spied through a gap and they were just as dead as I was but, unlike them, my mission was to narrow the field of vision, to reduce the space for those who would read them. It's a mistake to judge us as having condemned writers. Those red lines and blue crosses were dedicated to the readers, poor souls suffused with even more hope than those who sent me their texts, because writers come and go but readers are immortal; they are living, breathing individuals who believe in beautiful, everlasting stories. But, little by little, I narrowed the gap through which we spy the invisible universe.

You and all the others will no doubt find me despicable. To all of you I represent the hand that lowers the eyelid, blinds the eye, and leads – *led* – you into the darkness. But it wasn't the work of my hand. Good God, no. It was already long in existence. In fact, it has always been there. But if you're being sincere, Joan, you can't say I'm any more deserving of scorn than some of our esteemed colleagues, many of whom are much younger than I am and positioned much closer to the light. But it's a light they turn away from purely out of convenience and self-interest. They have no reason to be frightened and yet that is exactly what they are. I pity them. They dress their fear of passion up in strict, inflexible words. They no longer tell stories, nor do they know how to laugh. Oh sure, they laugh at me, of course they do, but that is an easy, complacent laughter lacking in joy. Genuine laughter has an altogether different rhythm: it has to be spontaneous. Just like when our girls laugh without even knowing what they are laughing about.

I can hear the teachers professing with phoney trepidation: here is the story of a mediocre Spanish literature teacher, with a despicable past, who paid the bills by censoring books! They discuss my wife and then, in more detail, their own, but always with the same incidental tedium with which they refer to me. Ah! Let them get on with it. When death draws near, one no longer has the will to turn the laughter of others into compassion. This is one of the benefits of getting old.

Some of these colleagues, as you and I have noted on more than one occasion, like to amuse themselves by toying with the girls, for there is so much admiration contained in young flesh! Of all the sins, vanity is the most venial. The women these men label as insipid are the ones who know their kind the best. Girls admire and flatter grown men because they are yet to know them. They smell mature, masculine skin the same way that we, in the throes of adolescence, became submerged in sweeping landscapes without examining what we saw. Later you learn to love differently, better, because past a certain age, love becomes nauseating. Oh, how sweet the comedy of young love!

But they don't want to think about any of that. They are laughing at me in the meeting, at an old teacher who never earned the respect of his students or his colleagues, caught red-handed spying on a group of half-naked little girls through the gap in a door. Of course they don't want to think about it: they can still enjoy such comedies. Certainly the most elegant and genial among them and, naturally, there is a lot of deception and posturing in pedagogy. Because when you have a young, willing body in your arms, which neither avoids nor shows you any unease, you feel everything is capable of starting anew. Rather, you want everything to start anew, just like my father did when the girl from the travelling circus rode him, her long hair flowing down.

I've never known how to start anew. I'm too much like the girl on the flying trapeze: a lepidoptera copying the forms and tones of an oak leaf, or camouflaging itself against a tree trunk, nothing but a disguised butterfly adapting itself to the gaze of others. I am what others want me to be, in exchange for them not hunting me down. Only my eye is free. My eye is neither incidental, nor mediocre, nor mortal. I govern through my gap, selecting the space through which I want to look. When I saw my father underneath the circus girl I sensed that my power would reside in my eyes. I still do it to this day: I narrow them and that vision of love returns to me, a love that knows full well that one day it will die. I reinvent that image of authentic love – authentic because it was so recklessly defiant.

Whenever I traced a red line through those beautiful, everlasting stories written by strangers it was as if I were erasing the gaze of a man who had discovered how to love. By supressing the words of others, I supressed my own memory, and for that reason I considered myself the model civil servant. I was better equipped than anyone to sniff out subtle insinuations and suggestions, to go beyond hunting vulgarities, so easily snared with even the most cursory of looks. I saw far beyond the written word, and so I informed my superiors. I could erase what was there without it even being there for I was capable of abolishing the absence that the imagination seeks to fill. And I could do it because it wasn't unknown terrain for me. I had seen. I wasn't like so many other civil servants, chaste out of a sense of duty, attending Mass and taking daily communion, only releasing the accumulation of repression and inhibition when clandestinely reading officially prohibited books. What about a former co-lleague (who shall respectfully remain anonymous), recently deceased? Performing his duty to the Catholic Church by fathering a child every year didn't stop him from secretly enjoying a bit on the side…

When I returned the typescripts to their authors, fat and bloated with red lines and blue crosses, they must have thought that I – the Mysterious One – was a creature who rebuked language and longing out of brutish ignorance. But they were mistaken: only he who has known has the power to punish. Children, for example, never censor.

I was loyal to the laws laid forth by my superiors, many of them over-nourished and the picture of piety, whose double lives not only enabled them to climb the ladder of influence but also to grease their palms while doing it. These were by no means sad, repressed men. How could they be when they didn't have a shred of conscience? This is something our younger colleagues also get wrong. They are much sadder and repressed than these men ever were because they lack the level of cynicism necessary to lead a double life. Prohibition enabled my superiors to flourish because if one doesn't prohibit one cannot sell at the highest possible price. Make it illegal and the price of vice goes through the roof. Did you know, for example, that an eminent colleague of mine who used to take tea every Thursday afternoon without fail with His Excellency, the Archbishop of Barcelona, was responsible for circulating illegal pornographic novels?

But I was just a subordinate. I was the fanatic my superiors needed, the puritan, as K says, who had allowed his longings to pass without being satisfied. That was why they also despised me: I believed in what I did. With each red line I destroyed yet another part of the ego that had once infinitely multiplied upon the rippling pool in the river bend. I destroyed my primitive desire to be multiple people at once. I destroyed the storyteller in me. By mutilating the beautiful, everlasting stories, I amputated one of my own limbs and cut off my own air supply, reducing the multiplicity with which we are born, until the years left me with nothing but a sparse, minimal biography.

Ultimately, I destroyed my desire to become another via the act of inventing fables. An effective censor must cease to find it desirous. Those at the top made the laws and I followed them to the letter. But, as I've already said, I was only the executioner's assistant. An executioner need not have faith in what he does. But his assistant must. Executioner's assistants are the public servants of the kingdom of darkness, for they are the ones who draw the blinds and switch out the lights. The perfect murder can only take place if there is someone there to contemplate it.

I'm going off topic again. And you are still waiting – if, indeed, you are still reading this – for an explanation of why I hid myself in the changing room cupboard to spy on the girls as they got undressed. No, I wasn't blinded by passion. That you would no doubt find more excusable, am I right? Nothing but an old man with one foot in the grave ogling chaste Susanna as she prepared to bathe. But let me tell you this: the little Susannas of today are no longer chaste and I don't have one foot in the grave.

Everything would have been different if they had only understood why I'd read K's poem to them. All I wanted was to feel myself capable of transmitting emotion again.

Before condemning them to oblivion, I was a man in love with words. As a boy, I read insatiably, but nothing of those readings has remained. I have no memory, remember? Informers and those who prey on images are prohibited from having one. I forgot as a means of survival. I forgot everything I had read, everything that had once guided me towards a coherent explanation of the world and led me towards another universe. In those days I went about apathetically teaching a bunch of boys bored out of their brains. One by one, my students and I ticked off the great writers, according to the textbook: Garcilaso, Rojas, Góngora... I did my utmost to speak as little as possible about

Cervantes. His game of mirrors and his mastery over multiplicity didn't suit my interests. Cervantes was a sinner who had learnt to forgive others for their sins only after first having forgiven himself for his own. They didn't care what I was explaining to them because I didn't care either. I was utterly indifferent. It was like a popular tune you have whistled so many times that you no longer even notice the melody, turning me into a hunter who couldn't remember the names of birds or a fisherman who had forgotten which fish are edible. I'd forgotten the mainspring of literature but that didn't stop me from teaching perfectly well. After all, nobody demands such knowledge from a literature teacher.

In the afternoons, I taught listlessly, but it was in the mornings, sat at my dismal desk in that dark room, when I really got down to business. All my concentration and energy went into my morning work. Obliterating words enabled me to realise my true identity, and a complete and solid self presented itself to me, free from apertures or fractures. In the afternoons, I merely repeated, month after month, year after year, the same lifeless comments made by others, which weren't exactly the key to any treasure trove of wisdom. But in the mornings... ah, in the mornings I was a destroyer! And then, in the afternoons, I'd repeat *ad infinitum* what my predecessors, the famed censors of yesteryear, hadn't been able to destroy in their day. Literature is like a waterwheel turning infinitely through the ages, driven by lethargic bodies such as mine and those of my students.

Art is only dangerous when it excites a person in a precise time and place thus, for that very reason, my students and I came to a tacit understanding: we'd remain indifferent at all times. Literature paces and sways behind the iron bars of the text book, encircled by the prolonged yawns of teachers and their students. Erase the arousal caused by a word that always appears unique, despite meaning the same as others, and words are learnt in much the same way as chemical formulas: to be forgotten at the earliest opportunity. Don't be shocked by what I am about to say but I sincerely believe there is no greater enemy of words than a literature teacher.

I remember the day I held K's poems in my hands for the first time. Those lines came to me too late in life. *Not for timid bodies was this fervour's pleasure made.* Would that violently illuminating chandelier fit in the tiny room of my body? As I've already explained, I took K's poems home with me, devouring them in a single night. Beside me my wife slept, just as my mother had all those years ago.

I'm now aware that by informing on my father I informed on myself. I couldn't, from that point onwards, transgress any law. In the process of informing, the informer commits an act of violence against himself and, leaving himself devoid of secrets, he ceases to invent stories. I began asking myself when this self-denial first took hold and, more to the point, how some random poem could have affected me so profoundly. I accepted that life would never grant me another of its radiant mornings. And that is when I remembered my father's words as he was walking out the door:

'Don't deny yourself like I've denied myself, son. Listen to your body and do everything you can so that someone, whether it's a man or a woman, listens to it with you. And in return be sure to listen to theirs with them."

Whether it's a man or a woman… He'd never spoken to me like that before. Why did he choose to do it just as he was about to leave for good? What wisdom did he take with him? At that precise moment, my vision of the gypsy girl changed. She became a boy swinging high up on the trapeze. Or maybe an angel? What new possibilities, what new ways of being, did that circus herald? Yet, more to the point, what was I doing in a circus out in the sticks when I was a city boy, born and bred, having grown up on a narrow street in one of Barcelona's oldest neighbourhoods? Now I understand everything: we all harbour within a similar fantasy to the one of the girl from the travelling circus. I'd rejected a genuine image, the one of my mother and father turning their back on me to embrace and love one another, and if I'd been capable of rendering that distant vision of authentic love into words – like the words mutilated by my own hand – perhaps I wouldn't have ended up a ridiculous contemplator. By denying my parents' love, I denied the existence of love, and by denying the existence of love, I denied myself.

You see, don't you? I'm doddering and getting it all wrong. But I'll continue in the only way I know how. It wasn't my father who told me to listen to my body: it was a poem. Or rather, it was my interpretation of a poem. I read in it what I subconsciously needed to read in it, and this tiny act returned me to the reader I used to be, long before I began to forget, long before my job behind a dark desk as far from the window as it was possible to be. K's verses excited me and, in doing so, they returned me to innocence.

K's poem carried this story to me upon the winds of imagination. My father wasn't my father but an unexpressed, unrecounted longing. What all those typescripts, sent to me by innumerable strangers over the years, never managed was achieved by one short poem read in the middle of the night.

Yes, the informer inevitably commits an act of violence against himself. With the help of all those stories I erased K's poem. But I was also steadily erasing the infinity of my multiplicitous ego as it rippled over the water towards the edges of a fictitious pool. All I retained was a single floating image, the saddest one, the one that they demanded of me.

VI

It's been years since I've been able to feel anything. I've been made entirely of air, the element of apathy. But before I even began I was already an expert in denying sex. On one occasion, my superiors demanded an explanation for why I hadn't engaged the red end of my double-sided pencil to eliminate some offensive sentence or put a colossal blue cross through some dangerous paragraph, as the law clearly stated, and consign to oblivion some impermissible offence towards the armed forces, the Motherland or the Catholic Church. Simply put, I hadn't seen them. They weren't talking about my rippling ego or exploring the absence of longing. I'd become an empty room where the sad chandelier had long since been switched off and not a single sound stirred. Their so-called patriotic sentiment or national pride didn't mean a thing to me. If I belong to anything it's to my memories, the ones from before the great parenthesis, back when I was capable of embodying each of the identities contained within me. I could have lived anywhere on Earth and it wouldn't have made any difference because I'll always be an outsider. Symbols don't move me in the slightest and I'm content to leave them to the masses and their leaders, those reprehensible characters capable of whipping the former into a frenzy for their own gain. Nor have I ever been a man of the church. The inexistence of God came to me as a negative epiphany one night as I lay below a rock, engulfed by a cloud of stars. My vision of the universe and its infinite grandeur got smaller the larger the microscopic, personalised fantasy of my father underneath the girl from the travelling circus became. The immense and the miniscule had joined as one. God and the tiniest particle had momentarily come together before evaporating into the void. And, naturally, I found myself alone, there between the biggest and the smallest, because the certainty involved in such situations never admits company. God didn't see me because he wasn't there and never again will he be there. But I found that I could become God by shutting myself in a cupboard and playing out the only identity left to me: that of the contemplator who spies on little girls as they get undressed.

I remember when the all-boys schools first began admitting girls. They turned up with the torpid elegance of adolescence that neither shirks risk nor fears death. They behaved as if they had always shared a classroom with boys and, in doing so, wiped out with one, simple gesture all those years we were only able to survive by forgetting. I saw my circus girl in all of them; they all had long copper hair and appeared to rise up as if wanting to burst through the roof and soar through the sky. They sat without moving, yet they flew. They sat without speaking, yet they laughed. They were alive. When they gazed back at me it was as if they could read my thoughts, detecting in them the distant image of a satisfied man reclining in a circus wagon. The image of the original fabulist. They knew everything. They recognised in me the longings that had passed without being satisfied. My mind was possessed by them, by all those little trapeze artists sat before me, by their innocence which, like all innocence, was false because it had been created by those who have long since ceased to be innocent. I wanted all those gypsy girls to know what they meant to me. I wanted them to forget the set texts of the curriculum and let me take them gently by the hand and guide them towards the gates of the kingdom of language where words flew freely. Words that would tell them, the inauthentic adults of the future, and me, an inauthentic adult in the present, beautiful, everlasting stories.

And that is how I came to be reading K's poem to them yesterday morning. I didn't tell them who it was by, only that they really listened to me:

Like the beautiful bodies of those who died before growing old,
sadly shut away in a sumptuous mausoleum,
roses by the head, jasmine at the feet –
so appear the longings that have passed
without being satisfied, not one of them granted
a single night of pleasure, or one of its radiant mornings.[*]

I finished reading and looked up at my students. At the boys

*Translation by Edmund Keeley and Philip Sherrard

and girls. But the distant looks on their faces told me they hadn't heard a single word. Those verses weren't required reading and, as such, they knew better than anyone they wouldn't appear in the final exam. The whole class was one giant, synchronised yawn. Those at the front openly displayed a bored, distracted air, while the ones at the back were giggling and throwing scrunched up pieces of paper at one another. It was the one time in all the years that I've been drifting along as a teacher that I attempted to give them something of my own. And I gave it to them in the form of a poem. A poem written by a master builder of words. That was all: a slice of my life converted into art and which wasn't on the curriculum. A little piece of my story contained within a poem by K.

I don't blame them. It's not their fault. It was already too late for me. Words had forsaken me. They had disavowed me because of how I'd tortured and abused them, because I refused to listen to them while there was still time. And now, in the absence of words, all that remains is the eye of the contemplator spying the world through the gap in a cupboard door, the eye of a ridiculous man not yet tired enough to die and who was incapable of keeping a secret to himself in order to recount it later on.